Meet the officers of the
Alaska K-9 Unit series
and their brave K-9 partners

Officer: Criminal psychologist Mallory Haru

K-9 Partner: Koko the Malinois

Assignment: Rehabilitate Koko while working with tech guru Eli Partridge to stay ahead of killers

Officer: Ian McCaffrey

K-9 Partner: Aurora the German shepherd

Assignment: Help forensic scientist Tala Elko track down a murderous ring of thieves

Maggie K. Black is an award-winning journalist and romantic suspense author with an insatiable love of traveling the world. She has lived in the American South, Europe and the Middle East. She now makes her home in Canada with her history-teacher husband, their two beautiful girls and a small but mighty dog. Maggie enjoys connecting with her readers at maggiekblack.com.

With over seventy books published and millions in print, **Lenora Worth** writes award-winning romance and romantic suspense. Three of her books finaled in the ACFW Carol Awards, and her Love Inspired Suspense novel *Body of Evidence* became a *New York Times* bestseller. Her novella in *Mistletoe Kisses* made her a *USA TODAY* bestselling author. Lenora goes on adventures with her retired husband, Don, and enjoys reading, baking and shopping...especially shoe shopping.

CHRISTMAS K-9 PROTECTORS

MAGGIE K. BLACK
LENORA WORTH

LOVE INSPIRED SUSPENSE

INSPIRATIONAL ROMANCE

Special thanks and acknowledgment are given to Maggie K. Black and Lenora Worth for their contributions to the Alaska K-9 Unit miniseries.

LOVE INSPIRED SUSPENSE

INSPIRATIONAL ROMANCE

ISBN-13: 978-1-335-72276-8

Christmas K-9 Protectors

Copyright © 2021 by Harlequin Books S.A.

Holiday Heist
Copyright © 2021 by Harlequin Books S.A.

Alaskan Christmas Chase
Copyright © 2021 by Harlequin Books S.A.

Recycling programs
for this product may
not exist in your area.

This edition published by arrangement with Harlequin Books S.A.

For questions and comments about the quality of this book, please contact us at CustomerService@Harlequin.com.

Love Inspired
22 Adelaide St. West, 40th Floor
Toronto, Ontario M5H 4E3, Canada
www.LoveInspired.com

Printed in U.S.A.

CONTENTS

HOLIDAY HEIST

Maggie K. Black

To Dianne and all of you spending Christmas alone.
Thank you for picking up this book.
I hope you enjoy reading it as much as I did writing it for you.

These things I have spoken unto you, that in me
ye might have peace. In the world ye shall have tribulation:
but be of good cheer; I have overcome the world.
—*John* 16:33

ONE

As forensic scientist Tala Ekho reached for her gingerbread latte at the busy Anchorage mall coffee kiosk, she had the unsettling suspicion that the person standing at the counter beside her was trying to get away with a crime. Even though it had been over an hour since she had clocked out of work, traded in her white lab coat for a festive Christmas sweater and even braided a red ribbon through her long black hair, her keen mind continued to analyze the data around her as if it was still inspecting clues at the Alaska State Crime Lab.

Tala's nose detected the pungent smell of isopropyl alcohol wafting off the slender woman's form, despite her obvious attempt to drown it out with a rather flowery perfume. Her long and puffy green coat was zipped all the way up and an oversize, furry hood hid her face. This was despite the fact that the mall had decided to turn up both the heat and Christmas carols to full blast.

Slight burn marks on the woman's fingers implied she'd recently tried to use a cigarette lighter to melt something, while bright splashes of yellow and red dye trapped in the creases of her fingernails meant it had likely been an ink-filled clothing security tag.

She felt the clues come together to create a complete picture. Analysis: the woman had tried to melt a security tag, it had exploded and so she'd doused herself with a heavy-duty cleaning alcohol to remove the evidence. There was no way someone would just bring a pungent cleanser like that to a mall in their purse without a very good reason.

Conclusion: she was a thief who'd come to the mall prepared to shoplift.

Just this morning, Tala had been briefing the Alaska K-9 Unit via video chat on evidence found at the recent armed robberies of two jewelry stores and a pawnshop. One of the elderly men working at the pawnshop the night of the robbery had disappeared, too, and still hadn't been found. Although the brazen perpetrator of the robberies had been identified by witnesses as a man—dubbed the Golden Bandit by local press—and armed robberies were a very different type of theft, one of the troopers had mentioned in passing that the Anchorage police were also on the lookout for a very pernicious shoplifter. The team had debated the possibility that the shoplifter and Golden Bandit were linked somehow but discarded it as unlikely.

Was the woman beside her the shoplifter her colleagues had been talking about? If so, what should Tala do about it?

The suspect moved away from the counter and over to the wall. Tala hesitated awkwardly, then sat at the closest empty table and dropped her purse on top, where it toppled over, spilling out a stack of green flyers for a donation drive at the hospice where her grandmother had died. She shoveled the flyers back in. For all the years Tala had spent in the lab poring over case evidence sent to her by the Alaska K-9 Unit, she'd never actually done any fieldwork—let alone tried to stop a criminal. She knew the law well enough to know she could hardly call security just because someone looked and smelled funny, and if she called her colleagues, the woman might be long gone by the time they arrived.

Help me, Lord. I need Your wisdom.

Tala pushed her silver-rimmed glasses up higher on her nose with one finger in the same motion she'd used countless times when examining evidence at the crime lab. The suspect appeared to be texting someone now, and there wasn't a security guard in sight.

Then a flash of periwinkle blue caught Tala's eye, and her heart leaped. There was a uniformed state trooper in the jewelry store talking to someone behind the engagement ring counter. She'd have assumed it was about the Golden Bandit case if he also hadn't been holding up a rather large ring. Well, it looked like someone was planning on proposing this Christmas. Judging by the young, long-haired and exceedingly fluffy German shepherd at his feet, the man was a rookie and not someone she'd worked with before. That said, she usually only saw the team through phone calls and video chats. She stood up to get a better look and saw he was tall, with a strong set of shoulders and a shock of short red hair. The trooper turned as if sensing her gaze and it was like the busy world around her froze.

It was Ian McCaffrey.

He'd aged over fifteen years and grown a tidy beard since she'd last seen his face at the disastrous high school party that had finally ended their friendship once and for all. That night they'd been arguing about the fact that she thought his hockey friends were bullies, then somehow she'd ended up blurting out that she liked him and they'd almost kissed before he turned tail and ran. They hadn't spoken since. But it was most definitely him—the guy who'd been her best friend from kindergarten and whom she used to think she'd one day marry.

Wow. Ian was a *K-9 trooper* now? His eyebrows rose as he scanned her face. But there was no time to begin to analyze this unexpected complication, because the suspected shoplifter was on the move again. The woman wove through the tables with her, unzipped her coat with one hand and then tripped, sending her phone clattering to the floor behind a crowded table of teenage boys in high school hockey jerseys. Tala noted the boys had name-brand electronics bags crowded around their feet. The woman bent down, scooped up her phone with one hand and slid something Tala couldn't quite make out into her open coat with the other. Then she straightened up and kept moving toward the exit, doing up her zipper as she went.

The shoplifter had just stolen something from one of the boys! Tala was convinced of it.

Lord...what do I do? I'm not a cop, but I have to do something. She's getting away!

If Tala was wrong, she was about to make a gigantic fool out of herself. But if she was right and didn't intervene, she'd never forgive herself. She leaped to her feet.

"Hey! Ma'am!" Tala yelled. "I think you just took something that isn't yours!"

The woman didn't stop moving, but her shoulders twitched as if she'd heard her. Tala glanced toward Ian, pointed at the shoplifter and hollered, "That woman just stole something!"

Ian's brows furrowed. Tala didn't wait for him to act. She scooped up her purse and jogged after her, feeling her boots slide on the wet floor.

"Excuse me!" She reached out and touched the woman's sleeve. "Ma'am! I saw you rob those boys!"

The suspect spun and yanked her arm back so suddenly Tala lost her footing and wiped out on the floor. Snorts of laughter rose from the table of teenage boys.

The woman's hood fell back, showing the immaculate makeup and pale blond pixie cut of an attractive woman probably in her late thirties. She was impeccably dressed and wearing a voluminous scarf worth at least what Tala earned as a month's salary.

"Hey, you! Officer!" the woman shouted and Tala turned to see both Ian and his K-9 partner running toward them. Heat rose to Tala's face. "This lady attacked me! Arrest her! *Now!*"

Of the dozens of things that Ian McCaffrey had never forgotten about his beautiful and brilliant former best friend was that Tala absolutely hated being the center of attention. So, as he watched her spring to her feet, defiance flashing in her dark eyes, he found himself silently praying that she wouldn't notice the crowd of people gawking at her now.

Then he added a second prayer for wisdom.

Give me strength, Lord. I barely feel prepared to face Tala again in the best of circumstances, let alone like this.

His late grandmother had always joked that the red-haired McCaffrey men were all heart and no brains. There was enough of a kernel of truth in it that he'd secretly debated whether he'd really be cut out for a job in law enforcement. Right now, his heart was pounding a mile a minute and his mind didn't know what to think.

He crossed the floor toward the two women, oddly thankful for the reassuring bulk of his K-9 partner, Aurora, by his side.

"Ian McCaffrey, Alaska State Trooper." His voice rose as he raised his badge aloft before sliding it back in his jacket. "What seems to be the problem?"

"She's a thief." Tala spoke first. "I'm sure of it. She smells like isopropyl alcohol, and she has burn marks on her fingertips and ink splatter on her cuticles."

She said the words with such confidence it was like Tala expected him to know what all that meant. A ferocity filled her gaze, radiating a confidence that somehow made her even more attractive than she had been when her mere smile had knocked his socks off back in high school.

Ever since he'd joined the Alaska K-9 Unit, he'd heard person after person tell him about the incredible forensic scientist who'd been an invaluable part of so many investigations. While he'd been steeling himself to face her again, he'd never imagined it would be in a moment like this.

"She just crouched down behind that table," Tala added, pointing with an outstretched arm to a group of teenagers who were both watching and recording the unfolding scene like it was the funniest thing they'd ever seen. "I think she stole something from one of those guys."

Ian fought the urge to roll his eyes as the hockey-jersey-clad teens patted themselves theatrically as if Tala's claim was all some big joke instead of actually looking through their bags to see if she was right. It was bravado, he guessed, the kind that made adolescent boys all join in on doing something dumb together instead of being smart and doing what was in their own best interest. He'd been the goalie of the same team in high school and some of his fellow teammates had practically competed to see who could act like the bigger idiot.

The well-dressed woman snorted.

"Is it true? Miss…" Ian dragged out the last word, hoping she'd supply him with her name.

"Claudia Mailer," she said. "And no, of course it's not. It's ludicrous and she's a menace." She fired off two rapid texts to someone Ian noticed was listed in her phone as "Boyfriend." Then she turned to Tala. "There's something seriously wrong with your brain, lady. You had no right to harass me like this. My boyfriend's got the money to hire a good lawyer. You should be glad I don't have time to stick around and press charges."

"Trust me, Ian," Tala countered. "She tried to melt a security tag, it exploded and she cleaned the ink off her hands with the alcohol. You can smell it. You can see it." Her dark and earnest eyes fixed on his face, through her glasses with round-wired frames. "And if she took off her jacket right now, I'm sure you'd see the ink splattered all over her."

His heart told him to believe her, but he also knew better than to trust it even as Claudia shoved her hands deep into her pockets.

"Did you actually see her steal something?" Ian asked.

"No," Tala admitted. "But all the data indicates it."

A ripple of whispers went through the watching crowd. Almost everyone had their cell phones out, either typing on them or—even worse—filming the altercation. The situation was deteriorating rapidly and it definitely sounded like the crowd was not on Tala's side. Ian heard a voice shout his name and looked over to see the jewelry store saleswoman he'd been talking to, jogging down the hall with a middle-aged security guard.

I could really use some help here.

Ian looked at Aurora. The long-haired German shepherd sat beside Tala and Aurora's shaggy face looked up into hers. Hmm. Apparently his K-9 partner had already chosen sides.

"Please, Ian," Tala said. "Remember how my

brain gets? It's always analyzing every little thing. I can't shut it off. But it's almost always right."

He wrenched his eyes away from her and breathed a silent prayer. Then he remembered he already had all the information he actually needed. It didn't make any difference what had happened when they were teenagers. Tala was his colleague now and she was very well respected by his new team. That was all that mattered.

Ian pulled his badge to show the approaching security guard.

"Trooper Ian McCaffrey," he said. "K-9 unit. This is Tala Ekho of the Alaska State Crime Lab. She has reason to believe this woman has been shoplifting. I realize this whole thing is a bit unusual, but Miss Ekho is an extremely skilled forensic scientist. Her expertise is valued by the Alaska K-9 Unit, and if she believes this woman here has been stealing, that's reason enough to detain her for questioning."

He blew out a hard breath, feeling like he'd oddly dodged a bullet. It wasn't personal; it was professional. No matter what weird twisting and turning his gut might be doing.

Claudia's eyes widened, and she sputtered a string of curses under her breath, as if she was completely and utterly shocked that Ian hadn't taken her side. Then she turned on her heel and strode quickly toward the exit. In an instant, the security guard was in hot pursuit, shouting at her to stop. The guard grabbed for her shoulder, and she spun back.

A bright yellow electronics-store bag slipped from inside her voluminous jacket and clattered to the floor, followed by a hot pink one from a cosmetics shop and a gauzy scarf that still had an anti-theft security tag on it.

"Hey! That's mine!" One of the hockey teens shouted and leaped to his feet. "She stole my new phone!"

His friends laughed and some other shoppers started clapping. Ian turned away. He'd never liked watching people celebrate somebody else's misfortune. It was too much like high school.

"Thank you." Tala turned to him.

"Colonel Lorenza Gallo told me personally how much she values your opinion," he said. "Several other Alaska K-9 Unit team members have, too. It was nothing personal. Any one of my fellow troopers would've done the same. Plus, you know, my dog, Aurora, totally believed you."

He meant the last bit as an awkward joke. But something dimmed behind Tala's eyes.

"Right, nothing personal," she repeated softly. But while the exact same words had sounded positive in his head, they now seemed completely different coming from her lips.

"Hey, officer lady, that was amazing!" shouted one of the teenager boys who'd been snickering at her just moments earlier. "How did you learn to solve crimes by guessing? Are you like Sherlock Holmes or something?"

"No," Tala told him. "Just studying plus experience."

There was an odd edge to her voice that reminded him of the way she'd reacted whenever any of his friends made fun of how hard she'd worked in high school. Back then she'd been so dedicated to learning she'd stay up all night hitting the books. All the while, he'd been completely focused on hockey and involved in playing for the team. Sure, some of the other guys had gotten caught up in stupid stuff. But he'd never been a part of it and didn't understand why it had bothered Tala as much as it did. It had grown even worse when the coach, who was a friend of his father's, had taken Ian under his wing and helped him apply for sports scholarships. He'd hoped she'd be happy for him. But after a while she wouldn't even come to the games.

Kicker was, he hadn't even gotten a scholarship.

"Why didn't you sic your dog on her?" another teenager asked.

"Aurora is a cadaver dog," Ian explained. At least until he convinced his boss she should be cross-trained. He ran his hand over the dog's shaggy head. "She only tracks dead people."

He'd been nineteen when a college classmate

had gone missing on a winter camping trip. Despite the tragedy of her death, he'd never forgotten the peace and closure it had brought to her parents when a K-9 cadaver dog had found her body in one of Alaska's abandoned gold mines. That memory had left a lasting impression on his heart and given him a calling to the sometimes-underappreciated K-9 work of finding those who'd died and bringing them home. But while Aurora had excelled at her training, Ian had been wondering whether he should ask his boss if Aurora could be cross-trained in another specialty.

"Excuse me, Officers!" A tall, blond man in his midforties, with a condescending frown on his brow, shouldered his way through the crowd. "Are either of you working on the Golden Bandit case? Because you'd like to think if the police are just arresting people on magic guesswork now, they'd actually be doing something about Anchorage's real criminals." He glanced around the crowd as if he was more interested in having an audience than talking to anyone in particular. "Did you know that the Golden Bandit has hit both a pawnshop and two jewelry stores in the past month? He stole a rather expensive golden necklace I'd purchased from one store and had left there to have engraved as a Christmas gift for a special friend. Surely the Alaska troopers would agree that a thief who'd stolen hundreds of thousands of dollars of merchandise is a higher priority than a petty mall shoplifter?"

Ian's back stiffened. That wasn't a question, it was an *indictment*. It frustrated him to no end that a local newspaper had given a serious criminal such a ridiculous nickname. And, unfortunately, it had stuck. This man had no idea how deeply Ian cared about stopping the string of violent break-ins, especially as a spate of similar unsolved crimes in Juneau last year had led to the disappearance of two pawnshop workers, on top of the elderly pawnshop employee who'd vanished in Anchorage recently. As much as he wanted all three found alive, he couldn't shake the fear that he and Aurora might one day find their corpses.

He had grown up in Alaska's gold-finding community. Anchorage was one of the few places so dedicated to it that their police department had a pawn detective, who'd been coordinating with Ian on this case. Both his father and late grandfather were metal detection enthusiasts and had close connections with pawn and jewelry shops across the state—who were usually the ones that both verified and bought the coins, rings, necklaces and lumps of raw gold people found. *This* man, however, with his furrowed brow and disapproving tone, had no idea how personally Ian took this case.

While a lot of people he knew still scoured

Alaska's abandoned mines for forgotten gold, Ian loved searching for recently lost treasures and returning them to their rightful owners. In fact, the whole reason he'd popped into the mall before his night shift began was to see if any of the jewelers could help him return a rather large emerald engagement ring that he and Aurora had found while hiking in the woods.

"So, are you assisting Trooper McCaffrey on the Golden Bandit case?" the jewelry store clerk asked Tala.

Ian half expected Tala to bristle at the subtle implication she was some kind of sidekick. But instead her chin rose.

"Obviously we can't give out specifics about ongoing cases," Tala said. "But yes, the Alaska State Crime Lab has been analyzing the evidence found at the scenes of the crimes while the state troopers chase investigative leads. It's a team effort."

A smile that was confident in a very reassuring way crossed her lips. It was the kind of expression that said there wasn't a doubt in her mind this case would be solved. It was really attractive.

The security guard still had the shoplifter standing off to the side. He waved Ian over. Ian glanced at his watch. It was just past six thirty and his shift started at seven. He turned to Tala and lowered his voice.

"I've got to go talk to the security guard and

also call Lorenza to let her know that I'll be late logging into my shift tonight," he said. "But please, wait for me and maybe we can grab a quick bite and catch up. It's been way too long since we talked, and I know that's probably my fault. But the Golden Bandit case is incredibly important to me and I want to clear the air if we're going to work together."

If he was honest, he also wanted to at least try to fix their friendship. But the way Tala pressed her lips together had Ian wondering if it was too little too late. Then Aurora licked his fingers, as if his K-9 partner sensed something was wrong and wanted to help but wasn't sure what to do. He wasn't sure, either.

"I should go. I just worked a ten-hour day in the lab," Tala said. "I only came here on my way home to pick up some flyers from a copy shop for a donation drive I'm helping with at the hospice that Grams passed away in. If I have time, I'm hoping to drop some off to them tonight on my way home."

Ian sucked in a painful breath. Tala had lost her mom when she was twelve and she'd never known her dad. Her grams had been like a second grandmother to Ian when they were growing up, and was all the family Tala had.

"I'm so sorry," he said. "My grandparents both passed two years ago, actually. They were in their home together until the very end."

"I'm sure they loved that," Tala said. "Your grandfather built a really amazing house."

"He did," Ian said. He'd also secretly mortgaged it late in life and left a lot of debt behind. "Do you still live at your grandmother's house?"

"Yup," she said. "Anyway, I really had enough of the mall for one day, I'm exhausted and I'm sure we'll see each other on a team meeting video chat soon."

The security guard was signaling him again. Ian raised a finger to say he'd be a minute. The man sighed and started escorting Claudia down the hall.

"Please, Tala," Ian said. "Give me fifteen minutes."

"I've got a bus to catch."

"I can give you a ride." His phone began to ring. "Please, wait here for me."

She didn't answer right away. He called Aurora to his side, then turned and strode down the hall after the security guard, in the hope Tala might be there when he got back. He answered the phone. It was his mom, triple-checking that he definitely wasn't bringing a surprise date to his parents' annual catered Christmas party fundraiser. He assured her he'd be coming solo. Then he ended the call, called his boss and quickly filled her in on what had happened at the mall.

Unfortunately, his visit to the security office wasn't settled as quickly or as easily. Claudia had resorted to loudly threatening to sue the security guard personally and the mall itself for a dozen ridiculous reasons and Ian felt obliged to stick around to make sure everything was okay until Anchorage police showed up to take over.

By the time he made it back to the food court, Tala was gone. His heart sank. Aurora butted her head against his leg.

"Thanks, girl," he said, looking down at his partner. "See, Tala and I were best friends once, a long time ago, and I ruined it." The German shepherd's ears perked as if she understood his emotions, if not his words. "We were at this party at my grandparents' house when we were seventeen and she said something really unexpected." *That she liked me and then we almost kissed.* "I panicked and she took it personally. I should've stepped up and tried to fix our friendship. But I didn't, because everything was just really awkward. She wanted me to quit the hockey team and hated my teammates. I was still hoping if I kept playing I'd get a scholarship. It was a mess and I still kick myself over it."

And now here he was, explaining the situation in hushed tones to his K-9 partner in a shopping mall. But to be fair, Aurora was a really good listener and talking to her helped somehow. Knowing Tala, he figured she would probably cut through the back parking lot and go through the industrial park to reach the express bus stop and knock half an hour off her journey. If he was right, they might be able to catch up with her.

"Come on," he told his K-9, "let's give it a try."

Ian and Aurora stepped out the back door into the snow. Thick flakes swirled around them. Although it wasn't yet seven at night, the sun had set hours ago. The mall's back parking lot was mostly just used for deliveries and was now completely deserted, with just a few dim pools of yellow lamplight against the blackness. He pulled his scarf up over his face against the cold.

A deep warning growl rumbled from Aurora's throat.

"What's wrong?" he asked. "Is it Tala?"

His footsteps quickened as they rushed around the back of the building and toward the adjacent lot. Bright green flyers for the Christmas drive were spread out across the ground ahead of them, in between fresh gashes that tire tracks had left in the snow. Her bag and its contents were also scattered haphazardly nearby. And, even worse, two pairs of footprints marked the clear sign of a struggle.

"Tala!" he shouted. "Tala, where are you?"

Something silver glinted on the ground in a pool of light. It was her glasses. Aurora whined.

"Ian!" Tala's faint and desperate voice floated through the snowy night. "Help me!"

TWO

"Shut up!" A gloved hand clamped down hard over Tala's mouth, stifling her scream. Her unseen attacker's voice was a harsh, male rasp in Tala's ear. "Not another sound out of you or I'll hurt you. Got that?"

She nodded, unable to see without her glasses as he propelled her through the dark and snowy parking lot, with one large hand on her face and the other hand on her back. Somewhere in the darkness, she could hear Aurora barking.

"Tala! Where are you?" Ian's shouts were so faint she could barely catch them.

Suddenly, she felt herself shoved against the cold, metal side of a van. The vehicle itself was barely more than a pale blur before her eyes, and the smell of blood filled her senses.

"Now, you're not going to cause me any trouble, are you?" her kidnapper asked.

It was a threat, not a question. She felt him yank her hands behind her back and tie them together with a plastic zip tie at the wrists. A van door slid open with a metallic screech in front of her. He thrust her forward and she smashed her shins against the frame as she fell into the van. The door slammed shut and a moment later, she heard him get into the front seat and start the engine.

She lay there on the van's freezing floor. Tears stung like ice at the corner of her eyes and her body felt so cold her limbs were numb. When the van began to move, the rumble of the engine seemed to reverberate through the vehicle and into her shaking body. She forced herself to take a deep breath in, prayed for God's help and exhaled as slowly as she could.

The air around her was so dark she could barely see, but she could tell she was in the back of a windowless van. One that had to be no different from the numerous other ones she'd analyzed forensic evidence from. She hadn't just pored over samples of DNA, weapons and drug residue, but also countless photos of the seats, walls, floors and door handles where they'd been found. A few months ago, crime scene investigators had even brought an entire van just like this one into the Alaska State Crime Lab and she'd scrutinized every inch of it, examining the minute data that would eventually lead to the safe rescue of a kidnapped child.

She'd never been the strongest, most coordinated or athletic person. Knowledge and experience had always been her best allies and she hoped they would save her now. She glanced at the front of the van. The back of her kidnapper's head was an indistinct shape hidden by the hood of his coat. He was alone and if she remembered correctly, his rearview mirror would give him very limited visibility. Also, unless the van had been significantly modified specifically to keep people in, it wouldn't have childproof locks in the cargo hold. That meant she might still be able to open the doors from the inside.

Tala rolled over to a seated position, dug her heels into the floor and pushed herself backward toward the sliding door until she felt it against her back. She gritted her teeth and inched herself upward until her fingers touched the door handle. Then she fumbled with the latch behind her, trying to picture it in her mind. While Tala might not survive a fall from a moving van, she knew it was better than waiting to see where her abductor was taking her.

"Hey!" The kidnapper's harsh voice roared. "What are you doing?"

Tala yanked the door open and her body flew backward out of the van. She landed hard in the thick snow, pain shooting through her core and the air whooshing from her lungs. *Thank You, God.* Tala forced herself to her feet and crawled over a concrete divider, knowing her kidnapper would be forced between following her on foot and driving around the long way. The pale glow of the mall lights shone ahead of her.

"Help me!" she shouted into the wind. "Someone's trying to abduct me!"

Was it her imagination or did she hear the faint sound of a dog barking?

She ran for the sound, seeing nothing but blurs of lights and shadows before her eyes. Then suddenly, she heard an engine growl, like some kind of motorized predator coming for her. The van swerved across her path, cutting her off. Tires screeched. A spray of wet slush hit her body. Then the van door slid open again like a mouth ready to swallow her whole. Her kidnapper leaped from the driver's seat. His form was shrouded in a hooded jacket and mask.

"I'm going to make you regret that," he growled.

Please! Save me, Lord!

"Tala!" Ian's strong voice cut through the snowy air. A ferocious howl rose to join his shout. "Can you hear me?"

"Ian!" she yelled. "I'm here! Help me!"

The masked man's gloved hand clamped around her wrist. Tala yanked back hard and swung her elbow around with a guttural cry and he fell back.

"I'm Trooper Ian McCaffrey of the Alaska K-9 Unit," Ian shouted, "and I'm ordering you to let her go!"

She ran toward the sound of Ian's voice and

Aurora's protective barks. The masked man caught her around the throat and hauled her back again. He dragged her toward the van.

"The attacker is male and at least six feet, with no discernible accent—" she shouted.

"Shut up!" Her kidnapper's other hand clamped over her mouth.

She bit it hard. He swore and let go.

"He's driving an unmarked and windowless van!" she yelled. "The back door opens at the side!"

The attacker's hand closed her mouth again.

"Listen to me," he rasped in her ear. "You will forget everything you think you know about the Golden Bandit. Stop digging. Destroy evidence and lie if you have to. Kill this case, Tala, or next time I will kill you."

How did he know that she worked for the crime lab?

He let go, so suddenly she felt her body collapse into the snow. She heard the van door slam and the vehicle peel off. Then she chocked back a sob.

"Tala!" Ian called. "Are you all right?"

She felt his strong arms reach for her as Ian dropped to the ground beside her. The warmth of him surrounded her as he pulled her into his chest. And at the same time, Aurora's soft fur pressed against her side, as if the long-haired German shepherd was standing guard over her. Ian's ragged breath, mingled with prayers of thanksgiving, filled her ears.

"Thank you," she said. "You saved me."

"Any time." Ian's voice was husky. "Are you okay? Did he hurt you?"

"I'm fine," she answered. "How did you find me?"

"I knew you'd cut through the back and take the express bus," Ian said. "We started walking that way, saw the signs of a struggle, found your purse in the snow and heard you scream. Do you want your glasses? They're in my coat."

When she nodded, he eased his right hand away from her shoulders and then slid her glasses onto her face. She blinked as the world around her came back into focus. Ian's fingers brushed against her bound wrists, and he sucked in a sharp breath.

"I'm so sorry," he said. "I didn't realize. Let me cut them free."

"We have to preserve the ties somehow, if we can," she said. "I've got nothing else to go on to track this guy and I don't want to destroy potential evidence. I couldn't see him. He didn't leave any DNA evidence. He...he knew my name and who I was. He told me to stop investigating the Golden Bandit." She turned in his arms and looked up at him. "Ian, what if that was him? What if that was the Golden Bandit?"

Ian's heart pounded like a drumbeat as he cradled Tala in his arms. He glanced into the darkness in the direction where the van had disappeared. Aurora's ears perked as if silently asking him if there was something she should do. He eased a hand from around Tala long enough to brush the back of the dog's neck, reassuring her that she was exactly where he needed her to be. Aurora turned and laid her head on Tala's chest. Her soulful eyes looked up into Tala's under large, furry brows. Ian swallowed hard.

"Good girl," he whispered. Then he turned to Tala. "Let me look at your wrists."

She nodded and he shone the light from his cell phone over them.

"Plastic zip ties," he said. "The good news is it'll just take me a second to cut them off."

"Bad news is there's not much hope for getting DNA off them," Tala finished this thought. "There are clean plastic baggies in my purse. You can put it in one of them."

He cut her hands free with his pocketknife and then fished her purse out from inside of his jacket and handed it to her. She pulled out a baggie and held it open while he dropped the thin strips of plastic inside and sealed it. Only then did she stand slowly, rubbing her wrists and looking around. He leaped to his feet. Aurora instinctively moved to Tala's side. Seemed his partner had excellent protective instincts.

"There's no point calling the crime scene investigators out here," Tala told him. "There's nothing to collect. Between the wind and the snow, I can barely even see the tire tracks anymore." He watched as she fired off a quick text and moments later read the reply. "The main crime scene investigator I normally coordinate with is Bob Flocks. He's a bit rough around the edges and his interpersonal skills leave something to be desired but he's incredibly thorough. He says right now the best we can do is take pictures and make notes, because there's no way they're pulling anything physical in snow like this. So that settles it."

"Got it." He got out his phone and snapped what he could of the area. While he was doing that, she found her phone in her bag and set it to record an audio note.

"The man grabbed me in a secluded part of the parking lot," Tala dictated into her phone. "He forced me to walk to his van. I couldn't see his face. He was wearing a jacket with a hood, gloves and a mask. I guesstimate he's over six feet tall. No distinctive regional accent. The voice and hand size definitely indicate he was a man." She paused a long moment, then added, "He smelled like blood. But I didn't feel anything wet or sticky in the van, and we didn't see any residue in the snow at the crime scene, so I don't know what that means."

She stopped recording.

"I can't say I'd have kept my wits about me

well enough to notice all that," Ian admitted. "Was the smell of blood in the van or on him?"

"On him," she said. "I think."

"Did he have a weapon?" he asked.

"I'm not sure. I don't remember him mentioning it. He basically overpowered me."

"He caught you by surprise," Ian said. "It could've happened to anyone. How did you escape the van?"

"I opened the door," Tala replied. "Vans like that don't lock people in unless specifically modified to do so."

"In the dark? With your hands tied behind your back?"

She shrugged. "I've analyzed the interior of similar vans before. So I conjured up a mental image of what the inside of one would look like and went from there."

"That's impressive." Ian whistled softly.

"I was distracted and unfocused when I left the mall," Tala admitted. "If I'd been paying better attention to my surroundings, he wouldn't have been able to get the jump on me."

She was blaming herself and it frustrated him, especially as he didn't know what to do about it.

"None of this was your fault," he said firmly. "I'm going to call it in now. Unless you want to?"

"Go ahead," she said.

He dialed Dispatch, gave them all the relevant information and then sent Lorenza a quick message, as well. He'd have a much longer conversation with his boss and his team as soon as he could. But for now, his heart was torn between the part of him that wanted to focus on every little detail that might help bring the Golden Bandit to justice and another, unfamiliar part that just wanted to hold Tala and make sure she was okay.

"What exactly did he tell you about the Golden Bandit case?" he asked.

"He told me to sabotage it. To stop digging, mislead investigators, ignore and destroy evidence. Basically, he told me to kill the case."

"So he knows who you are," Ian said, "and obviously he's scared of you and what you'll turn up."

Tala rolled her eyes. "Nobody's scared of me. I'm like the least threatening person alive."

"Are you kidding?" Ian asked. "You're brilliant." *And kind, thoughtful and stunning.* "I, for one, have always been intimidated by you."

She paused for a moment as if debating how to even respond to that.

"I need to go back to my office," she said. "Clearly, this man thinks I'll find something that can take him down."

"You want to go into work *now*?" he asked. The Alaska State Crime Lab was located on a rural road that backed onto a beautiful, forested ravine. It was also completely isolated. "Won't it be closed?"

"They officially shut at five," she replied. "But they'll be a security guard patrolling the place and I can get in with my key card after hours. I like being there alone when the place is deserted. It's quiet and peaceful."

Sure, it might be peaceful, but that didn't mean it was safe.

"I remember you always liked pulling all-nighters," he said. Just like he also remembered how he used to drop by in the middle of the night with food knowing that she'd have forgotten to eat. "But as you know, the body's reaction to trauma can be both unpredictable and delayed. Also, you'll be much sharper tackling the work once you've eaten something. I'm guessing you haven't had dinner?"

She shook her head. "No, but I'm not exactly hungry."

"I'm sure," he acknowledged. "But if you head to work alone right now and something happens to you I will never forgive myself."

"You're not responsible for me." Her arms crossed. "You've advised me. As a trooper and new colleague that's all that's required."

"Yeah, but that's not all you are to me, is it?" Ian's arms rose as if to catch the falling snow. "Tala, you were my best friend and the person I cared about most in the entire world. I know we haven't spoken in years. But are we really supposed to just be colleagues and act like none of that ever happened?"

"Well, we have to," she said tersely. "Otherwise, we need to tell Lorenza that we have a personal conflict."

When Lorenza had interviewed him for the K-9 unit, he'd told her how his late grandmother always joked the McCaffrey men were all heart and no brains. She'd reassured him that having a big heart could be a real asset to his work and his team, not to mention to his K-9 partner. But right now, he wasn't so sure.

"But you're correct," Tala said. "I could use a hot drink and I should probably grab food in case I'm hungry later. And we should also probably talk."

Despite how calm her tone was, an emotion he couldn't quite place quivered in her voice. Was she worried about the case? Her safety? Working with him? He was new to the Alaska K-9 Unit, and whether Tala realized it or not, catching the Golden Bandit meant a lot to him. Not just because he wanted to prove himself. But also because he'd grown up in the gold-finding community. And besides, he might be the utmost expert on the pawn and jewelry shops on the team.

Help me, Lord, I don't know how to fix what happened when we were teenagers. I don't even understand what happened between us.

Was he missing something? And if so, how would he keep it from impacting the case?

THREE

Fifteen minutes later, Tala stood in the ladies' room of her favorite coffee shop, gripping the counter so hard her knuckles ached as she tried to convince her reflection in the mirror that she was all right. But she still couldn't stop her hands from shaking.

She closed her eyes and prayed for peace.

Rationally she knew that she was now safe. Ian and his K-9 partner, Aurora, had come to her rescue and they were waiting for her just on the other side of the door. But the adrenaline coursing through her veins just couldn't be convinced. While Ian had lined up to get them drinks, she'd taken a few extra photos of herself in the mirror in case they were needed as evidence, then carefully cleaned every spot of muddy slush off her red wool coat with a wet wipe, before doing the same to her boots and bag. Afterward, she'd run a wet brush through her hair, washed her face and applied a little makeup. But nothing she'd done had been able to cleanse her mind of the irrational fear that when she opened her eyes again the masked man would be standing there over her shoulder.

How had Ian known that coming here was what she needed? If it hadn't been for him, she'd have been all alone in her office when the initial jolt of adrenaline-fueled denial about her feelings wore off leaving nothing but fear behind.

Not to mention that seeing Ian in the mall had thrown her for a loop. They used to call each other best friends because when they'd been kids that seemed like the most special label to give someone. But as she'd grown older, her young, innocent heart had secretly started to think of him as so much more than that and even dream that Ian would be the guy she'd marry one day.

Clearly, she was nowhere near as over him as she'd wanted to believe. Or the fact that he'd chosen his high school hockey friends over their friendship. Hadn't he seen how they'd treated her? The snickering behind her back? How they'd bump into her in the hallway and claim it was by accident? It had gotten even worse when she'd caught a couple of them trying to cheat off her test and told her history teacher, who also happened to be the hockey coach. Coach Charlie Heidorn was the kind of chill teacher who told students to call him by his first name and had promised he'd talk to the boys. But after that, it had escalated to wads of chewing gum flung into her hair from people who hid before she could spot them, swear words spray-painted on her grandmother's home and nasty anonymous notes wedged into her locker.

That was when she'd learned that knowing in her gut who was behind something didn't count for much if she didn't have proof. The coach and the principal had both believed her bullies when they protested they were innocent. And when she'd tried to talk to Ian, hoping he'd choose her over them, somehow she'd blurted out far more than she'd meant to. If only she hadn't almost kissed him. But she had, he'd rejected her and now they were going to be working together.

The door swung open behind her. Tala's eyes shot open as she turned to see an elderly woman in a blue shawl step through.

"Is that your doggie out there?" she asked, smile lines crinkling her eyes. "She's adorable."

Tala glanced past her and through the door as it slowly swung closed. There sat Aurora, at attention, with her ears perked and her back to the door as if she was on lookout.

"She's a friend's dog, actually," Tala explained, and Aurora's presence served as a reminder she couldn't just hide away clutching the fixtures forever.

"Merry Christmas," the lady said with a smile.

"You, too, Merry Christmas."

She stepped through the door and felt Aurora nuzzle her hand in greeting. Tala rubbed her fingers over the German shepherd's silky ears.

"Thank you for looking out for me," she whispered. "Now let's go find Ian."

Aurora woofed slightly and they started through the tables. Garlands and bows bedecked the crossing wooden beams above. The instrumental Christmas music playing through the speakers was slow and dreamy, and seemed to be a perfect match for the snow buffeting the window. This family-run coffee shop had been one of Tala's favorite hangouts since high school, when she'd spend hours hiding away in a corner by the fireplace studying.

She found Ian in that very spot waiting for her, in the chair across from her favorite one, where he'd sat while she studied so many times in the past. He stood as she approached.

"How are you?" he asked, running a hand over the back of his head.

"Shaken," she admitted. "But good. Thank you for sending Aurora to make sure I didn't get lost."

"No problem." He grinned. "She's pretty amazing and I feel incredibly blessed to be partnered with her."

Tala slid into her chair and looked down at the table. There was a hot green tea with lemon, peppermint chocolate mocha, three different types of grilled cheese and meat sandwiches, and a single cake pop. A smile brushed her lips. "You remembered all my favorites."

"I did." He sat and Aurora stretched out on the floor between their chairs.

"Then you'll also remember I can't eat this much," she said, "and you'll probably end up eating most of it."

"That was the plan." He chuckled. It was a warm and deep sound that seemed to finally melt the cold that had been coursing through her veins since the attack.

For a very long moment neither of them said anything.

"Your reputation with the K-9 team is absolutely stellar," he said, breaking the silence first. He leaned forward, rested his arms on the table and linked his fingers together. "I can't tell you how many of my teammates told me that while usually a forensic scientist only has one discipline, like weapons or biology, you've consulted on so many different types of cases you're invaluable."

"Thank you," she said. "But honestly, most of the time I only interact with the K-9 troopers through video chats or phone calls. We work out of two different buildings. There are a lot of people on the team I've never even met in person."

"Sounds lonely," he said.

"Does it?" she asked. Maybe it was. The members of the Alaska K-9 Unit were so close-knit they were practically family. It was only natural for her to feel like a bit of an outsider. "Well, I love the work and the entire team is wonderful. I'm sure you'll get along great with everyone. You were always great at fitting in."

Now, had that sounded bitter? She hoped it hadn't, but if it had, Ian didn't even blink. He really had no idea how hard it had been on her in high school when he'd suddenly become this hotshot goalie on the hockey team and been swallowed up in a brand-new group of friends.

They're teammates, not friends, Tala! Seventeen-year-old Ian's voice echoed in her memory. *I'm on the team for the hockey. I don't get involved in any of the stupid stuff.* From her perspective there'd been nothing but stupid stuff, like underage drinking and pulling stupid pranks. The girls who hung around the boys were just as bad. It had seemed like every other week Ian had a new girlfriend, who was the sister or friend of someone on the team. Then, to pour salt on the wound, Ian would drive Tala to school each morning and spend the whole trip dithering about why he thought he should break up with whoever he'd just started dating. Like he was counting on Tala to set his head straight!

"So, is the Golden Bandit the main case you're working on at the moment?" he asked, cutting into her thoughts.

"Pretty much," she said. "I remember your family was always big into metal detection."

"They are. And to be honest, so am I."

"You search for lost gold?" she asked.

"Recently lost treasures, more like," he said, and it was like a light switched on behind his eyes. "What I love is searching the glaciers, hiking trails and forests for things lost by tourists and hikers. There's nothing like reuniting someone with something they thought they've lost forever. Aurora's a great sidekick for that. That's actually what I was doing when you saw me at the mall. Aurora and I found an engagement ring in the woods, a really expensive, gaudy thing. I recognized the jeweler's mark and brought it in to see if they could help me locate the owner."

Oh! An unexpected sigh of relief slipped her lips. So Ian wasn't shopping for a girlfriend, then. His eyes widened like he could tell what she was thinking, and she felt a sudden heat rise to her cheeks. His phone began to ring. She looked down instinctively to where it sat on the table. It was Colonel Lorenza Gallo.

Ian stood as he answered. "Hello? … Yes, ma'am, Aurora and I are here with Tala … Okay… Got it. I'll be there as soon as I drop her off… Okay, I'll bring her with me. We're on our way. Bye."

He ended the call and she realized his face had paled.

"Sorry to cut this short," he said. "But that was the boss. We've got to go, and she wants you to come with us. Looks like the Golden Bandit has struck again and this time it's murder."

Less than five minutes later, Ian was pulling his SUV out of the parking lot. Tala sat in the passenger seat, balancing a take-out tray piled with drinks and food on her lap, while Aurora lounged in the back seat.

"I've never actually been to an active crime scene before," Tala confided. "That's the job of Bob Flocks and the other crime scene investigator. Not a forensic scientist. Do you know why she wants me to come?"

"No clue," Ian said. He felt his brow furrow as he watched the windshield wipers battle heavy snow. "My guess is that either she wants your insight on something urgent, or that she doesn't want me stopping to drop you off. Either way, I'm guessing it's pretty serious."

"Can you quickly tell me everything you can about the Golden Bandit?"

"Why?" he asked. He glanced at her and silently thanked God to see she was finally eating something, even if it was his favorite of the sandwiches. "I doubt I know anything you don't."

"Maybe not," she said. "But your perspective will be very different from mine and that's what I'm interested in."

"All right, then." He tightened his hands on the steering wheel and focused his gaze on his headlight beams as they cut a path for him in the darkness. "Well, first off, I hate the fact that everyone calls him the Golden Bandit. It's a silly nickname for someone who's stolen tens of thousands of dollars' worth of jewelry, antique coins and raw gold."

Not to mention Ian suspected the fact that three pawnshop workers had gone missing meant the bandit also had blood his hands. But suspicion wasn't the same as proof.

"You know that Anchorage is one of the few places in America that actually has a pawn detective whose full-time job is to work with pawnshops and secondhand jewelry?" Ian asked. "His name is Hugh Bertram. I don't know him personally, but he seems incredibly professional and thorough."

He realized he'd just used almost the same adjectives Tala had to describe the crime scene investigators she worked with. So much talent, yet so few leads.

"See, I actually didn't know that," she said. Maybe the fact that they had different perspectives on the case would be an asset. "Why would police dedicate one detective's entire workload to just pawnshops?"

"Melting down jewelry for raw gold is where the biggest profit is," Ian explained. "That means a lot of crime evidence gets completely destroyed and melted down by pawnshop owners and jewelers before police can find it, let alone seize it."

"So thieves use jewelers and pawnshops to launder stolen treasures?"

"Basically," Ian said. "Crime is rampant on cruise ships especially, because all thieves have to do is pop off at the next port and find a pawnshop to melt it for them. So Alaska slapped some very strict laws on pawnshops here. They have to hold on to anything they receive for two whole months before selling or melting it, to give the authorities the opportunity to trace if any of it was stolen. That's where Hugh comes in."

Red and blue flashing emergency lights cut through the squalls ahead. There were far more than he'd have expected to see at a crime scene. A shiver ran down his spine. He took a deep breath and decided to trust her with his suspicions.

"Also," he confessed, "my gut tells me we're dealing with the same criminal who hit all those jewelry and pawnshops in Juneau last year. I've got no proof but if I'm right those two missing pawnshop workers could be victims of foul play, along the one who went missing here, and we're dealing with a serial killer."

"But why attack a forensic scientist to try to stop the investigation?" she asked. "Why not just take the money he'd stolen so far and move on somewhere else before the cops move in?"

"I don't know," Ian admitted. "Maybe he can't walk away from that much money."

He drew closer and the pawnshop came into view amid the mass of emergency vehicles, including those of state troopers and local police, and ambulances. It was on the very end of an unassuming strip mall, with stores to the left and forest to the right. Two local officers were cordoning off the area in yellow crime scene tape, while others instructed the jostling crowd of spectators to move back. The flashing lights of emergency vehicles illuminated the shattered glass of the front store window and the remains of ripped Christmas garlands hung from the window frame like some kind of eerie vines. By the look of things, someone had hurled a display case of large and gaudy costume jewelry through the window, scattering the shimmering baubles across the snow.

Yeah, he could see how that might draw a crowd.

Then he saw the somehow both imposing and elegant form of Colonel Lorenza Gallo standing under the pawnshop awning in a long wool coat, with Trooper Poppy Walsh and her K-9 partner, Stormy. The mammoth wolfhound's head was cocked to the side as if she was taking in the briefing, too.

Tala's eyes widened in surprise. "Stormy tracks

live people and weapons. What are they doing here?"

"That's the exact same thing I was wondering," Ian said.

For that matter, why was a cadaver dog called to the scene?

The tall form of his colleague and recent mentor, Sean West, strode through the snow toward him, with his Akita partner, Grace, by his side. Ian rolled down the window and heard Aurora woof softly as if in greeting.

"What've we got?" he asked.

"Break and enter, robbery with a suspected double homicide by the look of it," Sean said. "But we really don't know."

"Suspected?" Ian echoed.

"Well, we've got a whole lot of blood," Sean said. "But no bodies."

FOUR

As Tala looked out the window at the scene unfolding around them, she felt an odd and unfamiliar knot twist in her stomach. Work in her forensics lab was orderly, logical and neat. No matter how violent, bloody or vile a crime might be, by the time the evidence reached her desk it was usually distilled down to a series of plastic collection bags, swabs, crime kits and photographs, with the odd random object or vehicle for her to inspect.

She hadn't been prepared for just how busy and chaotic a crime scene like this would be. Discordant lights flashed on and off from multiple directions at once, illuminating the broken glass, cheap jewelry and shattered Christmas decorations in the snow. Meanwhile, spectators shouted at law enforcement officers from behind yellow police tape, demanding information and trying to get better views for their camera phones.

"There are two separate blood trails disappearing into the snow in opposite directions," Sean went on. "At least two different people involved in the altercation took off on foot after whatever happened. We've got to find them."

"Got it." Ian nodded. "I'm guessing Hugh Bertram, the pawn detective, is in charge of the crime scene?"

Sean shook his head. "No, apparently nobody can reach him."

That didn't sound good. But Tala did not have time to ruminate on that, because Sean indicated where Ian should park. Ian got out, opened the back door for Aurora and signaled for her to join him. The German shepherd leaped to his side and stood alert and attentive as he clipped her leash onto her harness.

Tala followed Sean, Ian and their K-9 partners toward the pawnshop. She glanced through the broken front window at the wrecked display cases splattered with rust-colored blood and at the white-clad crime scene investigators moving between them. Something about it was off. Tala could sense it. But in that moment, she didn't know what. Ian lifted up the yellow police tape to walk under and then paused to hold the tape up for her.

"I've gotta go with Sean," Ian said softly. "Are you okay if I leave you here?"

His eyes met hers and something jolted in her

chest. She *wasn't* okay. But she also wasn't his problem to fix and he had a job to do.

"I will be," Tala assured him. She tried to smile and instead settled for what she hoped was a professional nod. Then she tucked her head under his arm and stepped inside the cordoned-off area. Ian dropped the tape, but he didn't move. Instead, they just stood there in the snow, inches apart from each other, with Aurora beside them.

"We still need to finish our conversation from earlier," Ian said gruffly. "My shift won't be up until tomorrow morning. Can I take you out for breakfast? Or even just give you a ride to work and we can grab coffee on the way?"

Tala couldn't help but notice that Sean had stopped a few paces ahead of them, like he was trying to give them privacy to talk while also trying to figure out what the relationship was between her and Ian. If they stood in the snow whispering to each other, Sean wouldn't be the only one. All that mattered right now was solving the case, she reminded herself. She couldn't let anything distract her or Ian from that.

"Thanks, but no," she replied. "But I'm sure we'll see each other on a group call very soon."

"Got it," Ian said stiffly. He turned and followed Sean and Grace across the snow with Aurora by his side.

Tala took a deep breath in and let it out slowly. Now what? The sense that something was wrong still nagged at her. She mentally analyzed every element of the scene around her until it hit her. Everything from the broken glass, to the crowd pressing behind the caution tape, to how local police were still securing the scene all looked so fresh and recent, she'd have pegged the crime as being discovered no more than twenty or maybe thirty minutes earlier.

So why then had two cadaver dogs been brought to the scene?

"Tala!" The warm and commanding voice of Colonel Lorenza Gallo, head of the K-9 unit and Alaska's first female K-9 officer, seemed to cut through the swirling flakes and chaos.

Tala jogged toward her, feeling unexpected relief to see the colonel. "It's good to see you."

Lorenza reached out her leather-gloved hands and clasped Tala's. "How are you doing?"

She gave the other woman a quick rundown of the kidnapping and the suspect, ending with the fact that she'd briefed Ian and taken detailed notes of the incident.

"Very good," Lorenza said. "I'm sure you've given us a lot to go on. But how are you feeling?"

"Overwhelmed and a bit numb," Tala told her honestly. "Also, very confused by all this."

"What do you find confusing?" Lorenza asked, with a look that was more curiosity than surprise.

"Look, I'm not a crime scene investigator," Tala started, "let alone a trooper—"

The colonel held up her hand before Tala could qualify herself any further. "Duly noted. Tell me what confuses you."

"Well, Grace and Aurora are cadaver dogs," she said, feeling slightly foolish to point out the obvious. "Studies do show that cadaver dogs can sense a deceased individual with ninety-eight percent accuracy within just three hours of death. Some theorize it could be even sooner than that." Lorenza's eyebrows rose. "But this crime scene seems pretty fresh. I can't imagine people drove by this pawnshop for hours without noticing the window was smashed. Most people would call the police immediately, and for the few that wouldn't, this place would be a looters' paradise." She released a breath, then continued, "Now, it's also true that dogs can smell what they call the scent of death for weeks after a body's been moved, as long as there are still residue particulates. Even if they're too small for the human eye. But then you'd need to suspect a dead body was here. So, why did you call out the cadaver dogs?"

The smile that turned at the edges of Lorenza's mouth gave Tala the odd sense she'd impressed her.

"Because the first officers on the scene could tell by coloration and scent that we were dealing with a mixture of both old and fresh blood," the older woman said.

"At the same crime scene?" Tala asked.

"In the same pools of blood," Lorenza clarified. "It's as if the Golden Bandit is trying to outsmart investigators by staging a crime scene where the timeline makes no sense. The store closed at five. Shouts were heard from nearby buildings and the front window was smashed around seven thirty, so a little over half an hour ago. But some of the blood was shed a couple of hours before that."

"I was forced into a van roughly an hour and a half ago," Tala said. "So, if it was all done by the same person—hypothetically—he started robbing the pawnshop after five, tried to kidnap me at the mall after six thirty and then was back here at seven thirty ransacking the place. The mall is only fifteen minutes away, so it's very doable. But again, that makes no sense. Usually, when a criminal returns to the scene of a crime, it's to clean it up, not make it messier."

A majestic howl sounded through the night. They turned to see Stormy charge out the back door along with her partner, Poppy. Tala wondered whose scent the wolfhound was chasing. Then Ian and Sean directed Aurora and Grace to sniff around the crime scene. Within moments both dogs signaled that they'd found a scent. Tala watched as the two K-9 teams headed out a side door and through deep snow up a hill toward the forest.

"I'd like you to don protective gear and take a

look around while the crime scene investigators are gathering evidence," Lorenza said. "I know you don't usually attend the scene itself and you'll get your chance to go over everything as usual when it arrives back. But officially, as the main forensic scientist on the case, I'm asking you to assess the scene to provide any added perspective."

"Absolutely," Tala said, "and unofficially?"

"This criminal has gotten away with multiple crimes without getting caught. And you've gotten closer to him that anyone else. So I'd appreciate your eye on this. Not for anything in particular but just because, in my experience, you've got an interesting way of looking at things."

Despite the cold, Tala felt a gentle heat rise to her cheeks. "Thank you. I'll do my best."

She whispered a prayer, steeled her breath and walked through the snow to the pawnshop, careful not to step on any broken glass or jewelry. Then she showed the Anchorage police officer guarding the door her officer crime lab ID. Nodding, he waved over a female officer who helped her into her full-body protective gear, including a white jumpsuit, facial mask and plastic gloves. Then she entered the pawnshop, feeling like an astronaut stepping through the door into an alternate world.

The store seemed to be divided into two display rooms. The one that she was in right now was entirely filled with glass cases, all of which had been smashed open. Rings, necklaces and tennis bracelets mingled on the floor with watches and antique coins. Had the Golden Bandit left in a hurry? Was he only after certain pieces? Judging by the size of the cases, he'd stolen a lot more than he'd left. According to white placards with numbers written in black marker, the cases had once displayed items priced anywhere between twenty dollars and several thousand. Tala knew she wouldn't have been able to tell at a glance which was which. But she wondered if Ian could.

She stood back and watched, careful not to get in the way or disturb any evidence, as crime scene investigators in white gear moved efficiently and methodically around the space, taking pictures, collecting samples and setting down small, numbered placards to show where things had been. It was fascinating.

She moved into the adjoining room. It was longer, narrower and filled with things less valuable than the square room was, like used sports equipment, large toys, a bin of DVDs and old electronics. At the far end lay the side door that Ian, Sean and their K-9 partners had disappeared through. Nothing in the room looked like it had even been touched, let alone rummaged through.

Then she saw it—the faint remnants of a familiar-shaped snowy footprint by the door, heading into the store. She pulled out her phone and checked the tread pattern against the picture she'd taken of the footprints in the parking lot at the scene of her kidnapping. It was hard to tell from what little remained of both, but they definitely seemed similar. Did this mean that the person who'd tried to kidnap her had been here?

A speck of something green caught her eye. She crouched down lower. It looked like a small and flattened spruce tree needle.

"You're not supposed to be in here." The gruff and annoyed voice of Bob Flocks came from behind her. "Do you need me to call someone to escort you out?"

She straightened up and turned. The head crime scene investigator was in his early forties, tall and handsome in that scruffy and perpetually irritated way that gritty television shows seemed to think a lot of women were into.

"Oh, Tala!" he said, with a surprise she couldn't tell was real or feigned. "Colonel Gallo did tell me that she wanted you admitted to the crime scene. I just presumed you'd check in with me."

Had he, now? She fought the urge to roll her eyes and reminded herself there was a lot of ego and pride in crime work.

"Nice to see you, Bob," she said. "What's your assessment of the scene?"

"Two people were in the store after closing time," he told her. "There was a fight. Knife, not gun. They ran out in separate directions."

She nodded. Well, she'd see what her own analysis turned up and if it confirmed or denied his theory.

"What were you looking at?" he asked curiously.

"What looks like a snowy footprint and a spruce needle," she said. "The footprint pattern reminds me of the tread in the pictures I took when I was almost kidnapped."

Bob took a step back as if suddenly realizing he'd been so focused on preserving the integrity of his crime scene that he'd forgotten to ask how she was after her ordeal. He raised his gloved hand protectively over her shoulder as if to mime patting her reassuringly without contaminating their gear.

"How you holding up?" he asked. "Look, if you ever want to grab a coffee and talk or anything, I'm here for you."

Now it was her turn to blink. Guess a damsel in distress brought out the crime scene investigator's gallant side. She couldn't remember the last time a man had asked her out for coffee. And today there'd been two.

"Thank you," she said. "Do you think we can get this needle taken back to the lab?"

"Honey, you know there are a hundred and twenty million acres of forested land in Alaska?" he said. *One hundred and twenty-nine million, actually.* "But sure, we can do that."

"Thank you," she said again. She glanced back down at the footprint.

You told me to wreck the case, she silently told her kidnapper, *and that only makes me more determined to do whatever it takes to make sure you're caught.*

Ian's long legs ploughed through the thick fallen snow. Fresh flakes beat down against his head. Ahead of him, Aurora bounded in long and confident leaps. Beside him, Sean was doing his best to keep pace with his K-9 partner, Grace. He guessed they'd been chasing the invisible scent trail for at least ten minutes, if not more, climbing deeper up the forested hill as the lights of the pawnshop crime scene grew smaller behind them. And yet, Aurora had continued unwavering to pursue whatever it was that her excellent nose and fellow K-9 both sensed.

Suddenly, the two dogs pulled to a stop in unison, Aurora barked urgently and Grace howled. Ian shone his flashlight down on the snowdrift at his feet and a shiver brushed his spine.

"Well done," he told Aurora softly. "Good girl."

Then he turned to his fellow officer, who'd just radioed Lorenza that the dogs had alerted. Thick flakes clung to the heavy scarf Sean had wrapped around the lower half of his face.

"Now what?" Ian asked.

"Now we dig," his teammate said, "and see what's there."

Whatever it was would be too sensitive to risk being damaged by dogs' paws, despite the expert diggers their partners were. The men crouched down and slowly swept the snow away with their gloved hands. Moments later, Ian felt his touch brush something. Sean sighed sadly, and gently brushed back just enough snow to confirm a man's dead body buried there, merely a few inches from the surface. Then he sat back on his heels.

"Lord, please help us catch whoever did this," Sean prayed.

"Amen," Ian agreed.

Sean stood and called it in. Ian stayed crouched beside the body. It was a young man in his early twenties, dressed in a bloodstained button-down shirt, jeans and boots. He recognized the face as a clerk at a pawnshop. Whatever reason he'd had for running out into the snow, he hadn't stopped to put on his gloves, hat or even coat. If the stab wounds hadn't killed him the cold would've finished him off. Ian found himself wondering yet again what had happened to the two young pawnshop clerks who'd disappeared from Juneau last winter. Then he felt Aurora's comforting bulk lean into his side and fill him with warmth.

"Backup is on their way," Sean said. He reached

down and helped Ian to his feet. "We've done all we can do. Now we wait."

Sean gently nudged Ian to turn his face away from the body and instead both men looked down the hill to where the paramedics, crime scene investigators, Anchorage police and troopers would be running up toward them. Minutes ticked past with neither of them speaking. Ian tried to take a deep breath, but his chest felt so heavy he could barely breathe.

"So, how do you know Tala?" Sean asked.

Ian wondered if his colleague was just making conversation to try to kill time and distract them both as they waited for backup.

"She was my best friend for a very long time," he said thickly. "Then we had a…"

A what? His voice trailed off as he tried to figure out a simple way to explain what had happened. Tala had been so much more than a friend. She'd been the most important person in his life and the one person in the world he could talk to about anything. The night of the high school party, they'd been standing alone on the side porch at his grandparents' house under the stars. She'd looked so unbelievably beautiful and his heart had ached to realize their friendship had been falling part.

She'd been so stubbornly convinced some of his players on the hockey team had it out for her, even though she'd had no actual proof, and they'd insisted to him they were innocent. He didn't understand how she could try to make him choose between her and hockey. Especially as he'd been hoping to get a scholarship to help pay for college.

Then she'd blown his whole world open by admitting she liked him as more than a friend. For a moment, he'd been too stunned to even speak. But then, as he'd leaned in to kiss her lips, the fear of what would happen if he messed it up, like every other relationship he'd had to that point, hit him like a fist to the gut and sent panic through his veins. He couldn't let himself kiss Tala because he couldn't let himself lose her friendship. Which might seem foolish in retrospect, but in that moment, he saw both playing hockey and his best friend slipping away. It was only then he realized that some of his teammates had witnessed the whole thing through the window.

"I don't know what to say," Ian said. "She was my rock and somehow I let myself lose her from my life. At the time all the reasons why seemed pretty important, but now I'm not so sure."

Sean nodded slowly as if hearing far more than Ian had actually said.

"Ivy was my rock, too," he said. A deep happiness bordering on wonder filled his voice as he mentioned his fiancée. "I lost her for a long time, but thankfully, God brought us back together. She's agreed to marry me again and we're adopting her foster son, Dylan, as our own. It's unbelievable."

Ian opened his mouth to tell Sean that it wasn't the same thing. He and Tala had never been in love. They'd just been inseparable.

Lights and voices rose, as law enforcement ran up the hill toward them. Ian and Sean stepped back to let the paramedics and officers do their job.

"Ian! Sean!" Lorenza called. "A moment?"

They followed the sound of her voice and found the colonel standing off to the side. Even in the darkness, Ian could tell in a glance the news wasn't good.

"Stormy picked up the scent of Pawn Detective Hugh Bertram," she said. "She and Poppy found him in a nearby alley. He was unconscious and has lost a lot of blood. Paramedics don't think he's going to pull through."

Ian let out a long breath. It was now even more certain that the Golden Bandit was a murderer and his sights were set on Tala.

FIVE

At two in the morning, Tala sat alone in the living room of the small two-bedroom house she'd inherited from her grandmother. Its emptiness seemed to loom around her, broken only by the sounds of Grams's bird clock ticking in the kitchen and heavy snow buffeting the windows. The house was dark except for a lamp by her side and the strings of twinkling lights she'd wrapped around the long leaves of the succulent plants on the other side of the room. Christmas lights blinked through the night around the birch trees in front of her house, making the curtains she'd pulled across the large front window flash from red, to green, to white again.

Normally Tala enjoyed the quiet. But now she wished she hadn't let the hospice keep her grandmother's zebra finches after her grandmother passed. Their little chirps and peeps would've been comforting on long nights like this when sleep failed her. But the birds were in the hospice's sun-filled living room, where they enjoyed the company of two resident cats and a dog. She'd left Grams's artificial Christmas tree there, too.

Lord, help me focus. Give me peace. Help me sleep.

Tala walked into the kitchen and considered going back to her laptop, which she'd left half-buried on the kitchen table, under newspaper articles she'd clipped about the Golden Bandit case. Instead, she put the kettle on and tossed two chamomile tea bags into her teapot. She took a long look out the back door at the snow cascading through the back porch light. Then she went back into the living room as the water boiled.

Thoughts of Ian weighed heavy on her mind. He used to perch himself on the front porch's top step and wait for her when she wasn't expecting him and barge through the back door into the kitchen when she was. Memories of him seemed scattered over every corner of the house, from the living room floor where they'd stretched out to play video games together, to the kitchen where they'd made copious amounts of popcorn, to the cupboard under the stairs where they'd hidden and read comic books.

A shadow passed by the front window. The lights changed from white to red. The shape loomed larger. It was the silhouette of a hooded man. Fear shot through her. The lights flashed again, and then, to her relief, he was gone. She stood there for one long moment, staring at the empty space where the shape of a man had been. Finally, she crept forward, slid the corner of the curtains back and looked outside. The front yard was empty.

Was she seeing things? Was she losing her mind?

Her cell phone began to ring, shattering the silence and sending her nerves jangling so hard she could almost feel them inside her. She searched the living room for her phone and eventually found it in the mess on the kitchen table.

The screen read "Unknown Caller," but that wasn't rare in her line of work. She suspected it might be Bob calling about the crime scene.

She hoped it was Ian.

She answered on the third ring. "Hello?"

"Hello, Tala." The voice was male and menacing, and she recognized it in an instant. It was the man who'd grabbed her, bound her hands and forced her into his van. She clasped her hand over her mouth to muffle a terrified cry from slipping out.

"You were warned what would happen if you didn't do what you were told," her kidnapper said.

Terror washed through her veins so cold that for a moment she couldn't move. *Come on, Tala! Think like a cop. You've got the criminal on the phone right now. What would Lorenza do?* She glanced to her laptop on the table. If she kept him talking and used her computer to contact the team, they could wake up Eli Partridge, the K-9 unit's tech guru, and get him to track the call and tell her what else to do. But for that to work she had to keep him talking.

And she'd always been much better at getting tongue-tied than small talk.

"Who are you?" she asked and heard her own voice quake. "What do you want?"

The kettle wailed so loudly for a moment she thought she could hear it echo down the phone. She ran and switched it off.

"Stop playing stupid, Tala!" he yelled so loudly that she leaped, sending scalding water splashing over the counter. "Don't insult my intelligence. We both know what a smart and special little girl you are and what I told you to do."

And if he really knew her, he'd know how much she hated being talked down to like that. She set the kettle down, feeling the sudden urge to punch this stranger right in the jaw.

"I know exactly what you told me to do!" she snapped so loudly she was almost shouting back. "You told me to destroy evidence and derail the investigation. What makes you think I can even do that? Do you even have any idea how a crime scene investigation works? I can't just single-handedly wreck one."

She strode across the kitchen, pushed the mess

of newspaper clippings off her laptop and opened the lid.

"Oh, I know exactly who you are, Tala Ekho, and what you're capable of with that special brain of yours."

That was twice he'd called her special and there was a certain venom to the word that felt intensely personal. He was so confident, too, even arrogant, that he knew exactly whom he was talking to. It was time she did, too.

"And you're the Golden Bandit, right?" she asked.

He chuckled. "It's got a ring to it, doesn't it?"

"I'll take that as a yes."

She switched her laptop on. It chimed as the desktop sprang to life.

"Don't touch that!" the Golden Bandit snapped.

He must've heard it through the phone. She winced and hit the mute button before her laptop could make another sound and let him know that she hadn't followed his order. Then she opened the email server.

"I told you not to touch your laptop!" he growled. "Step back from the kitchen table! Now!" The voice filled her ear and echoed outside the door. "You think this is a joke?"

Pounding sounded so hard on the back door it began to shake in its frame. She spun. A masked figure stood just feet away on the other side of the glass.

He smashed his fist against the window. It shattered.

The radio on the front dash of Ian's SUV crackled. The female dispatcher's voice came on. "All cars. There's a report of a break-in at 629 Rose Ave—"

Tala's house! Fear shot up his spine. He glanced at Aurora sitting beside him on the seat. The dog tensed as if sensing his fear.

"This is Trooper McCaffrey," he answered. "My K-9 partner and I are on it. We're four minutes away. Can you patch me in?"

"Her phone's gone dead."

He checked his blind spot and spun his vehicle in a tight U-turn, thankful that Lorenza had agreed to let him and Aurora patrol Tala's neighborhood and its nearby pawnshops in case of trouble.

Lord, please, help me get there in time.

He drove as fast as he dared through the empty streets bedecked with holiday lights. His phone rang with a call from the colonel. He ended the call with Dispatch and answered.

"Tala's in danger—" she started.

"I know," he said. "We're two minutes away—"

"Good. I'm sending Poppy and Stormy as backup."

The call ended. Ian reached the driveway and pulled in so sharply the SUV skidded to a stop. Then he leaped out and unholstered his weapon, signaling Aurora to his side.

"Hello!" he shouted and rapped hard on the door. "Tala? This is Alaska State Trooper Ian McCaffrey!"

Something about identifying himself as law enforcement at a home he'd cheerfully walked into hundreds of times before compounded the fear already building inside him. He kicked over the rock that Tala's grandmother used to hide a spare key beneath, found nothing there and then ran to the back of the house. A crash sounded ahead of him. Then he saw a masked figure dart out the back door and take off running through the woods. In a moment the figure was lost to the snow. Ian groaned, wishing the criminal had less of a head start, that he had backup to check on Tala while he chased after him, or that Aurora specialized in tracking and pursuing criminals.

Instead, he ran through the back door, which lay open with its window smashed. Broken glass and newspaper clippings littered the floor.

"Tala!" he called. "Tala! It's me, Ian!"

The living room didn't look like it had been touched. It took him two seconds flat to race upstairs, check out the house's small main bedroom and even smaller second one, before rushing back downstairs. Then he realized Aurora was sitting beside the small triangle-shaped door to the cupboard under the stairs. His partner's head was cocked to the side. He crouched down beside the door.

"Hey, Tala," he said gently. "It's me, Ian. The house is empty. The man who broke in is gone."

He heard a soft scraping sound, then the door opened and he saw Tala peer out from behind a pile of camping equipment. By the look of things she'd barricaded herself in and armed herself with a baseball bat.

"I didn't have time to run," she said shakily, answering the question he guessed was in his eyes. "I was standing just feet away from him when he smashed the back door window and I knew it would be just seconds until he got inside. My boots and coat were between me and him and I knew I'd be in even more danger if I ran out without them...so I grabbed my phone and my laptop and hid."

His mind flashed to the corpse Aurora and Grace had found buried by the snow. Tears burned his eyes when he thought of what could've happened to Tala.

Thank You, Lord, I don't know what I'd do if anything happened to her.

"Ian!" Poppy's voice sounded behind him.

He turned to see the red-haired trooper standing in the back doorway with her massive wolfhound filling the space. He pivoted on one knee to face her.

"House is clear," he said. "Tala's safe. Single suspect took off on feet through the woods heading west."

"Got it," Poppy said. Her eyes flickered to Tala's face for a moment and concern pooled in their depths. Then she and Stormy ran back out into the night.

He prayed and asked God to help them catch the Golden Bandit.

Then Ian turned back to Tala and watched as she unfolded her limbs and eased her body out of the small space. It was amazing to think they'd both used to fit in there and sit cross-legged, with their knees touching as they read comics together.

"Are you okay?" he asked, feeling something heavy build on the back of his throat.

"I don't know," Tala admitted. Her chin quivered. "Those flyers had my phone number on them and I dropped them at the mall."

He reached for her hand, she took it and he helped her out until she was crouched on the floor beside him. They hesitated there, eye-level with Aurora. He was just about to stand and help her up to her feet, when suddenly she said, "Oh, Ian, I was so scared."

Instinctively, he opened his arms and she tumbled into them. Her head fell into the crook of his shoulder. He held her tightly.

"It's okay," he whispered. "I've got you and I won't let anything happen to you. I promise."

Ian held her for a long moment, feeling her breath hitch and shudder against his chest. Then slowly, her limbs stopped shaking and her breath settled, but still they stayed there, holding each other. Then without saying a word she eased back slightly, just enough that they could look into each other's eyes. His hand slid down to the small of her back. Suddenly he felt that same overwhelming desire to kiss her lips that he'd felt back when they were teenagers. Only somehow deeper. He didn't just want to embrace her. He wanted to hold her, protect her and do whatever it took to keep her safe.

But when she pulled away, he reluctantly let her go and they both stood. She strode past him into the kitchen, suddenly all business, as if the tender moment between them hadn't ever happened.

"Once again I don't see much point in calling out the forensics team," she said. "My window was broken, nothing was stolen by the looks of it and he won't have left any DNA. Also, I really don't want the perception of special treatment just because investigators know me personally. It would be wrong. I want to be treated the same as any other break-and-entry victim. I'm not special."

There was something bitter in her tone when

she said the word *special*, almost like she thought it was an insult.

"The real question is how this man knows who I am and why he's so convinced I can single-handedly derail an entire investigation," she added.

"Did he say anything to you?" Ian hazarded a guess.

"The Golden Bandit?" Tala murmured. "Yes, he called my cell phone and threatened me from outside my house, before he broke in. He was toying with me, Ian. And I don't think he's going to stop until he gets what he wants from me."

SIX

Ian's arms longed to hold her again, but she was pacing now.

"He not only wants me to wreck the investigation," she said, "but he's supremely confident that I have the power to do so. He goaded me about how smart I am. All I can think is he's linked somehow to someone who was at the mall today when we stopped the shoplifter and heard me blurt out that I'm working on the Golden Bandit case. Claudia did text her boyfriend and she said he was wealthy. Also, there was that odd man who asked about the case and complained his necklace had been stolen."

"Or it could be that someone in law enforcement or the state lab is compromised," Ian suggested. "It's also possible that he saw someone post about it online. A lot of people had their phones out. The entire high school hockey team, for starters."

He practically had to force himself to stop

watching her and instead turned to looked over the damaged door.

"Good news is that it'll only take me a couple of minutes to hammer a piece of wood over the window," he said. "Then we can get the glass replaced first thing tomorrow. I'll see about getting dead bolts installed, too."

"Thank you, I appreciate that."

"You don't have to thank me, but you are most welcome." He grinned at her. "For now, how about you, me and Aurora set up camp in the living room? We can pop a ton of popcorn, make hot chocolate and watch old Christmas movies. It'll be just like old times."

"What happened at the pawnshop after I left?" she asked, like she hadn't even heard him.

"Sean and I found the body of the pawnshop clerk," Ian said, feeling the smile fall from his face. "By the look of things he'd been stabbed, then he'd run into the woods and died. Poppy found pawn detective Hugh Betram. He'd been stabbed, too, and was pronounced dead at hospital."

She gasped. "I'm so sorry to hear that."

"Thanks." He ran his head over the back of his neck.

"I promise, I'm going to do everything I can to catch his killer," she said. And he knew without a doubt that she would. "Can you drive me to the crime lab?"

"In the morning? Sure."

"No," she said. "Right now."

He blinked. "It's getting close to three in the morning."

"I know. But I've got a key card and there's a security guard at the front desk. It's not like I'm going to be able to sleep, and the sooner I process the samples that the crime scene investigators brought in tonight the sooner we'll start to get answers."

He knew she wouldn't be able to sleep and that Lorenza would sign off on him keeping her company in case the Golden Bandit came back. That was why he'd suggested they watch movies and eat popcorn. Instead, she'd rather go into work? Although he'd never have told her that, the fact that she was so singularly focused on studying had been part of why they'd grown apart. What guy would want to hang out in silence and watch her pore over books when he could be watching a movie or grabbing a slice of pizza after the game? But this was who she was. She'd worked for her career, she'd excelled at it and he wouldn't be much of a friend or a colleague if he didn't support her.

"Yeah," he said. "Sure, of course, we can do that. I'll just give Lorenza a call and let her know."

He had a quick chat with his boss, who told him that unfortunately the Golden Bandit had disappeared into a parked vehicle and driven off before Poppy and Stormy could catch up with him. Then Ian found some wood, hammer and nails in the shed and took care of the broken window. Tala came back downstairs after having changed into crisp professional slacks and a dark red cardigan sweater. Her long black hair was tied back in a tight bun.

He filled her in on what Lorenza had said about the Golden Bandit getting away. Then they drove to the Alaska State Crime Lab in near silence, except for light small talk about when the snow was due to break. He parked under a streetlamp in the nearly empty parking lot, across from a black truck he assumed belonged to the security guard. Then he harnessed Aurora and followed Tala. She used her key card to enter the building, waved to the guard at the front desk, signed Ian in and then used her key card again to access the elevator to her floor. At least security was good. They came out onto a long floor of office cubicles. There was a small meeting space that also seemed to serve as a break room, with two chairs and a couch. Then there was the lab, separated by a large glass wall, with floor-to-ceiling windows looking out over the parking lot.

"There's a coffee machine by the wall," she told him, "and also some chairs and a couch if you want to relax. I'm going to be pretty focused for a while."

"Don't worry about us. We're good."

A smile crossed her face and it was beautiful. She strode into the lab, exchanged her red cardigan for a white lab coat, then bent down and checked a medical evidence fridge. Meanwhile, he gave Aurora permission to lie down and relax as he stood and watched Tala move silently through the space. After removing an evidence bag from the small fridge, she set it on the stainless steel counters, sampled something on a small glass slide, looked at it under a microscope, checked her laptop and then repeated it all again with the next sample. It was like a dance without music. And she looked more content and relaxed than he could remember seeing her in a long time. It hit him that she'd finally become the person she'd been working so hard to become when they were younger. She'd gone from being teased by their idiotic classmates to being skilled, appreciated, talented and respected.

Lord, I don't know what else to say but thank You for letting me see who Tala has become.

The sky was still dark, when Lorenza called, hours later, to remind him that his shift was finally over, and he was free to clock out and go home, but that Tala had texted her to decline the offer of another backup officer. He waved at the glass to signal to Tala that he and Aurora were leaving, but she was so focused she didn't seem to notice. So instead, he lay down on the couch with his feet off the edge and waited for her to take a break. He hadn't realized he'd closed his eyes, let alone fallen asleep, until he heard Tala whispering his name.

"Ian, wake up."

He opened his eyes to see she'd pulled up a chair beside him. Soft wisps of hair fell loose from her bun.

"I didn't fall asleep on the job," he said quickly.

"I know." She laughed. It was an amazing sound. "Lorenza told me your shift was over. I would've woken you up sooner, but I figured you were tired and you both looked so comfortable."

It was only then that he noticed his partner was curled up in a surprisingly small and tight ball of fur beside him, with her nose hidden beneath her tail. Her ears twitched like radars monitoring the world outside her sleep. He reached over and scratched the back of her head.

"I both asked and prayed to be partnered with a cadaver dog," he said, "after realizing the peace and closure it could bring to people to bury their loved ones. But I've been wondering if I was wrong and maybe I should ask if Aurora could be cross-trained in something else." Huh, he didn't think he'd ever admitted that to anyone before. "Does that make me sound terrible?"

She pressed her lips together.

"No, it sounds…" Talia blew out a long breath as if recalculating her words. "I don't know quite how to say this. You were always the kind of guy who'd get really excited about something, then start second-guessing it and ask me to overanalyze it with you."

Unexpected heat rose to the back of his neck. Although she hadn't said it, he couldn't help but think she was referencing the number of wrong girls he'd dated in his teens.

She leaned forward. Light seemed to dance in her dark eyes behind her wire-framed glasses. "Now, I wanted to make sure you were actually awake before I hit you with this, but I found something."

"Then hit me!" He swung his legs around and sat up, careful not to disturb Aurora. But the dog woke immediately and sat at attention, as if she was also anticipating a briefing.

"First off, there was nothing usable from the fingerprints," she said. "It seems the Golden Bandit was wearing gloves. There was also no trace on the plastic zip ties he used on me, which isn't surprising, either. But I've found three distinct blood samples at the pawnshop. One belongs to the detective, the other I've connected to the pawn clerk, but the third is an unknown sample. It's also fresher blood than the other two. Ian, I can prove a third person was there, and we have his DNA!"

"Really?" Ian's back straightened. There was something electric about the smile that spread across his face. "You've isolated a third DNA sample at the crime scene? Wow, Tala, this is the break we've been waiting for! Now all we have to do is find the person who matches his DNA and we've got him."

"Hopefully," she qualified. "We have no idea who this third person is or what he was doing there. There've been no hits in the system so far. But his blood is all over the crime scene."

Ian let out a long breath, leaned toward her, grabbed both of her hands in his and held them. The edges of their knees touched.

"You're brilliant," he said. "You're absolutely amazing and you always have been. I could just…"

What? He could just what? But his words trailed off as if he'd realized what he was just about to say and stopped himself. He didn't utter anything more. Neither did she. Instead they just sat there, clasping each other's hands as silence filled the space between them.

Then something darkened in the green of his eyes, as if a new emotion, one she'd never seen before, swept through their depths. Whatever that look was, it was both gentle and strong, and somehow she knew it was a feeling that was safe to fall into and yet also so fierce it took her breath away. A cell phone rang, shattering the silence. They both leaped and checked their pockets, before she realized it was hers and she'd left it in the lab. She ran for it, fumbled as she grabbed it, knocked it on the floor and then picked it back up again.

"It was Lorenza." She glanced at the screen. "I think I hung up on her."

"You'd better call her back," Ian said. His partner whimpered slightly and nudged him as if very politely trying to get his attention. "I need to walk and feed Aurora. She's been extremely patient about sleeping in a forensics lab but it's time I took care of her. Especially as my shift technically ended a couple of hours ago."

"People will be arriving any minute," she murmured, turning to look out the window. "There are already a few cars in the lot."

"You want me to drive you home?" he asked.

She shook her head. "Thanks, but I've got a lot of work to do here."

Ian paused. Then he ran his hands down his slacks.

"I've got tonight off work for my parents' annual Christmas party," he said. "It's a late-afternoon and evening thing. If you're not doing anything, do you want to go with me? It's more of a fundraiser for local charities they're involved with. But it's a good time and I'm sure I can get you an extra ticket..."

Oh! Something unexpected fluttered in her chest. Yes, she remembered just how fun and special that annual Christmas party was when she was a kid, and how odd it was when at four-teen he decided to take another girl who he had a crush on instead.

"Yes," she said and felt a flush rise to her cheeks. "That would be great."

"Awesome!" Ian grinned. "I can pick you up at six if that works?" When she nodded, he went on to say, "As you know, my parents are really con-nected to the gold-hunting and metal-detection community. There will be a lot of people there who were impacted by the Golden Bandit. It's even possible the bandit himself will be there. This will be a great opportunity for you to use that brilliant mind of yours to home in on any clues or leads."

And just like that the happy bubble of joy that had been building in her chest deflated and popped. Oh, so it was not a date, then. But an undercover assignment of sorts.

"Yeah," she said quietly. "Sounds good."

She wasn't sure what the expression on her face looked like, but whatever it was, Ian's smile dimmed as swiftly as someone turning out a lightbulb. His mouth opened like he was about to say something more. But her cell phone rang again. She glanced at the screen.

"I should take this…it's Lorenza. I'll see you tonight. And thanks again for all your help."

Then she turned away and answered the phone.

"Hi, it's Tala," she murmured. "Sorry, I think

I accidentally hung up on you earlier. It's been a long night…"

Ian and Aurora were already walking away down the hall. She quickly filled Lorenza in on everything that had happened since they'd spoken last, from the break-in to finding the third blood sample.

"I have a request," the colonel said, and for some reason her voice became almost hesitant. "If it's all right with you, I'd like us to subtly spread the rumor that you're taking a break from the Golden Bandit investigation. Not that we're in any way actually removing you from this case," she added quickly before Tala could even open her mouth to respond. "But clearly, this criminal has set his sights on you and I'd like to lower your profile to make him think you're a less important target. For your safety, and also so that you can focus on processing the evidence without having to constantly look over your shoulder."

Lorenza was usually always so straight and direct that Tala had never actually heard her hedge her words before.

"Sounds good," she said. "I'm all for lowering my profile and getting this bandit guy off my back. I trust you to handle it however you see fit."

Lorenza blew out a long breath that Tala hadn't realized she'd been holding.

"Wow," the colonel said. "Thank you. That's refreshing. You wouldn't believe the amount of ego and pride there can be in everything related to this line of work."

Tala thought of how Bob had practically puffed out his chest and pounded on it at the crime scene.

"Have you slept at all in the last twenty-four hours?" Lorenza added.

"No," Tala admitted. To be honest, she actually hadn't slept in the past twenty-six.

"Then you need to go home and sleep," Lorenza said, "for the sake of the case and your work. It will not only help sell the story that you're taking a break, but it'll be good for you, too. You've already processed the blood samples and fingerprints and given my team a lot to go on. We all get sloppy when we're tired, including me, and we can't afford any mistakes on this case. We need you at your best, Tala. Got it?"

"Got it," Tala said. Not that she liked it. She didn't feel tired or hungry, just driven to push through. But the last thing she needed was for fatigue to smack her hard between the eyes when she was handling a delicate sample.

Lorenza sent Poppy and Stormy to give her a ride home. The auburn-haired trooper was just getting off an extended night shift. While Poppy still seemed to be shaking off her disappointment at the fact that the Golden Bandit had gotten away from them, her gigantic dog snored peacefully from the back seat.

Still, Tala could see the Poppy's shoulders

begin to relax and a smile spread across her face as conversation turned to Poppy's recent marriage to Park Ranger Lex Fielding. His little son, Danny, had been the ring bearer and walked down the aisle with Stormy.

Tala looked at the simple and elegant wedding ring on the trooper's finger. "Can I ask you a question?"

"Of course." Poppy pulled into Tala's driveway and turned to face her on the seat.

"How did you get over the fact that Lex hurt you in the past?" Tala winced. "I'm sorry if that's too personal. But my life is about studying evidence and last time you were engaged it didn't work out."

The other woman brushed her hair back from her face and smiled.

"Lex and I were different people back then," she said. "We both needed to grow and change. I'm glad we didn't get married then, because if we had we wouldn't have Danny now and we might not have become who we were meant to be."

Poppy's words ran circles through Tala's mind as she crawled into bed, planning to nap for an hour and then work from home on her laptop for a while. Instead, she passed out before she could even figure out what it was about what Poppy had said that niggled her, and then woke up to find the sun was already starting its trek back down to the horizon and that Ian would be there in less than half an hour. She paced as she got ready, picking and discarding multiple outfits and feeling every bit as nervous and on edge as she used to be when he picked her up as a teenager.

Finally, she chose a long red velvet top with a wide scoop neck and a lacey black skirt that fell just below her knees. She brushed her black hair loose around her shoulders in loose waves, braided a little up around the crown of her head and tied it back with a ribbon.

Tala fished out a fresh and unopened pack of disposable contacts. She hadn't worn contact lenses since she'd been a teenager hoping to get Ian to think of her as more than a friend. Then she got irritated with herself, threw them out without even trying to put them in and instead picked a pair of sparkling gold-rimmed glasses that she'd bought on a whim.

Ian's SUV pulled up in front of her house five minutes early. Not quite what she expected from a guy who never used to be on time. Her heart thumped with every step as she walked toward the door and opened it. "Hey."

There stood Ian in a dark gray suit and a bright red tie. His green eyes twinkled, and she realized that at some point during the day he'd managed to get his hair cut. He ran his hand along his jaw.

"You look good," he said.

"Thanks," she murmured. "Um...so do you."

"Well, I'm glad I guessed right that you'd be wearing red," he said.

Hang on, did he intentionally dress to make sure they matched?

A small polite whimper dragged her gaze down to his feet. There sat Aurora at attention, with a matching red bandanna around her neck and a pair of antlers on a headband perched on her head.

Tala laughed, so loudly and suddenly that she grabbed her mouth in embarrassment. "How did you get her to wear those?"

"I don't know," he said. "I just plopped the headband on her and she didn't try to shake it off."

Aurora smiled a wide doggie grin, like she was in on the joke. He stretched out his hand for Tala. She took it and let him walk her to the car. Then they drove to the party in near silence. Invisible nerves danced and jangled between them like wind chimes. It wasn't until he pulled off the highway onto a small country road that she realized he was driving to the house in the forest that his grandfather had built. Golden Christmas lights encircled large trees around the ranch-style house. Red and green ones wound up the pillars of the front and side porch, across the top and back down again.

"Your parents live here now?" she asked.

"We all do," Ian said. He eased the truck down

the long driveway. "My grandfather made a lot of foolish investments and left my dad tons of debt. My parents sold their house to help pay off the remortgage on this house and also cover his and my grandma's medical bills. But there's still a pretty big hole." A muscle ticked in his jaw. "It's been rough financially. I live here to help contribute. Physically, Dad's a big and strong guy. He's in his fifties, still lifts weights and runs triathlons. But emotionally, money problems have been really hard on him."

She thought about the house her grandmother had left her. Sure, it was tiny. But the mortgage was paid and her grandmother's meager savings had covered most of her end-of-life hospice care. The hospice's charity fund, which Tala was helping raise funds for, had covered the rest.

"I didn't have any idea your family was struggling financially," she admitted. They'd always seemed so wealthy.

Ian blew out a long breath.

"I only really found out when I started thinking about college," he said. "And that's when my dad pulled me aside and told me it would be good if I could get a scholarship. My grades weren't the best, so I threw myself into hockey, hoping I'd get a sports one, but it didn't happen in the end."

Huh. She felt something soften inside her chest. While that didn't change how his teammates had treated her, it did help her understand why he'd reacted so badly when she'd told him she thought he should quit the team. Poppy's words from the night before about how she and Lex had changed filled Tala's mind again.

She was being bullied, Ian had been worried about his family's finances, and they'd both been just kids dealing with some pretty adult problems.

"Also, I don't really know how to tell you this," Ian added, "so I'm just going to come out and say it. My parents think that we're more than friends...or at least that we're heading that way."

He stopped the car. The way his eyes darted every direction but at her made it pretty clear that "more than friends" didn't mean colleagues. Her heart skipped a nervous beat.

"You told your parents that we're *dating*?" she heard her voice rise.

"No! Of course not. But they jumped to that conclusion, and in all honesty, I didn't try too hard to convince them otherwise," he said. "You've got to understand that they run this event as a charity every year. This year the money's going to support the blood drive our old high school hockey team now does every year. The party is catered, they were expecting a certain number of guests who'd already confirmed, and I only sprung it on them today that I was bringing a date when I'd promised my mom just yesterday that I was coming solo."

"And Lorenza wants it to look like I'm stepping back from the Golden Bandit investigation," Tala said, trying to steer the conversation somewhere safer. "So it won't hurt to let people think I'm here as your *friend* and not because we're working together."

She stretched the word *friend* out a little longer than she'd meant to. Probably no one would even notice or care why she was there.

But that assumption faltered the moment they reached the front door and were greeted by Ian's parents, who immediately swept her up into a warm hug and told her how happy they were to see her. Then they moved into the front room with a large spruce tree decked out in the very same dried cranberry popcorn strings she remembered making with Ian when they were kids.

"I'm really glad my parents still went through with hosting this party," Ian whispered in her ear, "and that Dad's still doing charity work. There was a time I thought he was so stressed about everything he was just going to disappear into himself."

"Well, it's good he has you in his life," Tala said softly. "Nobody ever got me out of my own head like you did."

He smiled. "Ditto."

They moved deeper into the party. People mingled throughout the main floor and clustered around the living and dining rooms, balancing plates of party food. Most were around the same age as Ian's parents and there were many whom she recognized from work, school and the community. And while they were definitely quick to congratulate Ian on his new job with the K-9 unit and fawn over how adorable Aurora looked in antlers, definitely the warmest greetings, knowing smiles and welcomes were directed toward Tala.

"Why does it feel like everyone is way too happy about the fact that you and I are here together tonight?" she asked Ian under her breath as they browsed the dessert table.

Ian chuckled softly. "People are just being friendly."

Yeah right. There was warm Alaskan hospitality and then there was apparently outshining an incredibly cute dog in antlers.

"Or curious," she said. "Are people like this with every date you bring to the Christmas party?"

"I wouldn't know," he murmured back. He palmed a piece of sausage and passed it to Aurora under the table. "I haven't brought a date to anything like this in at least seven or eight years."

Well, that would explain why everyone was smiling at him like he'd just walked in with a unicorn.

"Really?" she asked. "But you're the guy who used to have a new girlfriend every few weeks."

"Yeah," he said, wincing, "and how did that work out for me?"

"Oh, wow, is that you Tala Ekho?" A deep, male and vaguely familiar voice rose above the din. "I barely recognized you!"

SEVEN

She turned to see Charlie Heidorn, their former history teacher and Ian's high school hockey coach, striding toward them. While she guessed he must be in his late fifties now, only the smallest touch of gray brushed his blond hair, and he still had the build of a man who hit the gym twice a day. He was flanked by two of the guys she'd worked hard to avoid in high school, Chip Costales and Barret Lasker, who'd both lost a lot of their athletic build but none of their swagger.

"You still friends with your former teammates?" she whispered, horrified.

So much for thinking Ian had changed.

"No, not really," he said. "But Charlie's a friend of my dad. He still coaches the team and my parents support the team's charity work. I guess he brought a couple of the guys from the old team."

Then he turned to face the other three men and there were complicated fist bump–style handshakes all around. "Thanks for coming and Merry Christmas."

"Wouldn't miss it for the world," Charlie said. His gaze turned to Tala, with a smile that brought to mind the term *charm offensive*. "Did I hear that you're a big shot scientist now? I always knew you were destined for greatness."

She felt Aurora's wet nose nudge against her fingers. She scratched the dog's chin.

"Forensic scientist, actually," she said stiffly.

Charlie's eyes widened and his head shook as if the thought was too wonderful to believe. "That explains it! Some of the kids on the team said you'd solved the Golden Bandit case."

Did they, now? Good to know teenage gossip was as accurate as always.

"Not at all," she told him. "I'm actually taking a bit of a break from the case."

Which was true, if she counted the fact that she'd spent most of the day asleep.

"Well, I called your lab today and spoke to your colleague Bob," Charlie said. "I wanted to bring some evidence by which might be relevant to the case."

Tala watched as Ian's eyebrows rose, and felt hers do the same.

"What kind of evidence?" Ian asked.

"I don't know if you remember my daughter, Millie," the coach said. "She was a couple of years behind you in school. Millie runs a mining-themed tourism business. Took it over from her husband last year when he tragically drowned in a boating accident. People come from all over the world to explore abandoned mines and try their hand panning for gold. There are always a few tourists each year who hit a sizable nugget. She even sells some of the smaller gold nuggets she's found on her website." He glanced around the room. "I'll make an appointment to drop by and fill investigators in more. Let's just say I have reason to believe her late husband might've been involved in something dodgy."

Tala remembered the boating accident vaguely. Millie had called her husband in missing after he'd gone boating alone. His sailboat had eventually been found capsized, but his body had never been found. But the coast guard had also waited over a week before calling in the K-9 unit to help with the search due to some suspicion her husband had just left her. Accidents like that were all too common in Alaska and one of the reasons Lorenza had increased the number of cadaver dogs on the team.

"You know if you want to see Millie's place I could take you up there sometime for a hike," Barret said. He leaned past the coach with a smile that practically oozed swagger. "Maybe take a picnic?"

She almost choked. Was one of the same guys who'd been irritated she wouldn't let him cheat off her in high school actually *flirting* with her now? She wondered if Ian noticed the weight of Barret's gaze lingering on her. Instinctively, she stepped closer into the handsome trooper's side. Ian's arm slid around her shoulder and Barret's eyes clocked it move.

"Oh, I'm sorry!" Barret laughed, a bit too loudly, like he'd just heard a joke no one else could hear. "I didn't realize you two were an item now. Wow, Ian, you sure have come a long way from that time back in high school when Tala tried to kiss you, you freaked out, called her a loser and ran away!"

Sudden heat rose to Tala. She felt nauseated and dizzy, almost like she had food poisoning. That memory was back. From the shock in Ian's eyes to how humiliated she'd felt as she'd run from the party and called her grandmother to pick her up.

The tiniest rumble of a growl built in Aurora's throat. Ian's hand slid down to the small of Tala's back and he pulled her closer to his side.

"Well, that's ridiculous," Ian said. "There is absolutely no way I ever called Tala a loser. And any man in his right mind would give anything to have this incredible woman at his side."

Then, before his former teammates could wisecrack any more, Ian gently steered her toward the large glass double doors that led out to the side porch and closed the door behind them. Snow spread out in front of them in an endless blanket of white, dazzling like diamonds. The sun dipped below the horizon, leaving a wash of pink and gold in its wake. She gasped a breath of freezing air, thankful for the cold on her face, and her nausea faded.

"Here, take my coat," Ian said. He pulled it off and draped it over her shoulders.

"No." She raised her hands to push him away. "Thank you, but—"

"*Please*, I insist," he said. "I know where the heat vent is by the wall and I'm really used to running around in the snow in my shirtsleeves."

She nodded. "Okay, thanks."

"Also, don't look now, but I wouldn't be surprised if people were watching us out the window." He draped it over her shoulders and then adjusted it. His hands lingered on the lapels. "You're shaking. You shouldn't let jerks like Barret get to you."

She stepped back just enough that the lapels tugged out of his hands.

"You have no idea what it was like for me back then," she said. "To be bullied by them."

"You're right," he said soberly. "I don't."

"It's like they went out of their way every day to make sure I was miserable and afraid," she said. "It wasn't just the times they bodychecked or tripped me in the hallway, or flicked gross things at me, or stuck horrible notes in my locker that hurt me. It was living every day on edge, never feeling safe and never knowing when they'd strike next. And, to make matters worse, even when I finally mustered the nerve to report them, I wasn't listened to."

"That's partially on me and I'm sorry," Ian said. "I should've stood up for you. Just because I never saw them pull that stuff in front of me doesn't mean I shouldn't have believed you. I was wrong and I'm sorry."

Emotion pooled in the depths of his eyes.

"Why did you tell Barret that you didn't remember the fact that we almost kissed?" she asked. "It happened right here on this porch."

What? That wasn't the way the conversation had gone at all!

He stepped back, just slightly.

"You kidding me?" he asked. "I never said that—"

"You said it was ridiculous—"

"Because the way he was talking about it was!" He felt his voice rise. Surely that's not how she'd remembered what had happened between them back then, too? "Yes, I remember that you got up the courage to admit you liked me, we almost kissed and then I ran away like a coward. But we *both* leaned in for that kiss, Tala. I never rejected you or pushed you away."

"You did!" Her voice rose and his eyes widened. He glanced toward the sliding glass doors and then he moved even closer than he'd been before. "You might not have called me a loser or physically pushed me, but you looked horrified."

His face paled. He rocked back on his heels.

"I'm sorry," he said. "Really, if that's how it felt, I apologize. But that's not how I remember it. I wasn't horrified, I was terrified. You were my best friend. You were the most important person in the world to me and I was terrified that if I kissed you, I'd start second-guessing myself like I always did and hurt you. I didn't think I could *survive* without you."

His warm breath mingled with cold air on her cheeks.

"Well, you chose your teammates over me," she huffed, "and seemed to have survived just fine without me."

His hand reached up and brushed the side of her face. And something about the simple touch sent an odd warmth coursing through her like dozens of tiny party sparkles.

"But I didn't mean to," he said huskily, "and I didn't want to survive without you. Losing you was definitely not the plan. I stupidly thought that I'd just run out the clock until I got that sports scholarship, then we'd leave high school and we'd go back to being friends like normal. I was wrong." He released a ragged breath. "I've thought a million times that if I could go back and be seventeen again, I'd wrap you up in my arms and kiss you. Because, sure I might've lost you just the same. Or maybe we'd have even fallen in love and gotten married. I don't know! But what I *do* know is that after all these years without you, that's a risk I wish I'd been brave enough to take."

Oh, Ian. He had no idea how much she'd wanted that, too. Her lips parted slightly but she couldn't think of anything to say. His hands slid around her waist and he pulled her close to him. She told herself that he was just doing it for show, that someone had to be watching and he didn't want to blow their cover.

But what if she was *wrong*?

"Do you want me to go ask the guys to leave?" he asked.

"No," she said. "It's okay. But thank you."

"Would it be okay if I kissed you now?" Ian asked.

She glanced to the window. The curtains had been drawn from the inside. No one was watching them. They were alone.

"Yes," she whispered.

He kissed her, tentatively and tenderly, like he was afraid she was a dream and he didn't want to wake up. She kissed him back, wrapping her arms around him, and he pulled her up onto her tiptoes. The warmth of him surrounded her and filled her core with an unfamiliar happiness that somehow felt like coming home to a place she belonged after being away for far too long.

The lights went out, plunging the world in darkness. Aurora growled loudly and they abruptly pulled apart. The K-9 was turned toward the window. Her ears were perked. Her hackles rose.

"What is it, girl?" Ian asked.

Then Tala heard voices screaming.

Ian unholstered his weapon. Aurora growled again and stood at attention, facing the glass door. He pulled the antlers from her head. Shouts of fear and trepidation grew from within his house. He slid the door open a crack, thankful that whoever had drawn the curtains had given him something to hide behind. For a moment there was pitch-black air and the sound of people panicking. Then a blindingly bright tactical light began to flash, showing staccato scenes of terrified party guests cowering on the floor.

"I'm the Golden Bandit, and this is a robbery!" The man's voice was as loud and rough as it was fake, as if he was intentionally trying to sound gruff. "Just do what I say, and nobody gets hurt. You're going to take off your rings, necklaces and bracelets, and put it in this bag."

Ian stepped back and let the curtain fall.

"Is that him?" he whispered to Tala.

"Sounds exactly like him," she said. That was good enough for Ian. "But the crime doesn't match anything we know about the Golden Bandit. He's never hit a party before. It's an escalation and a change in pattern. It doesn't make any sense that he'd do something like this."

No, it didn't, and that worried him.

Lord, please give me wisdom. My heart wants to burst in there and take him down. But if I just run in there and fire, I could be putting everyone inside in danger. He glanced through the curtain again, and this time forced himself to block out the fear and terror and resist the temptation to look for the faces of families and friends. Instead, he focused on the criminal, the crime and the facts. The first thing he noticed was there were no obvious signs of blood or injury. *Thank God.* Then he saw jewelry covering the floor as people practically threw it toward the criminal, and that the Golden Bandit was carrying a handgun.

"I want you to stay hidden and call for backup," Ian commanded. "I mean it. Promise me you won't put yourself in danger."

"I promise," she said softly. She brushed a furtive kiss over his cheek. "You and Aurora stay safe."

He pulled back the curtain again and waited, seconds passing by like minutes, until he saw the Golden Bandit holster his weapon so he could reach for his loot. Steeling himself, Ian stepped through the curtain with Aurora by his side, raised his badge with one hand and pointed his service weapon at the criminal with the other.

"Ian McCaffrey, Alaska State Trooper," he

shouted. "Hands up, drop your weapon and get down on the floor. Now!"

The Golden Bandit sent his blinding tactical strobe light spinning into the group like a grenade. Was he trying to give someone a seizure? Ian shielded his eyes, leaped for it and switched it off. But it was too late. Already his eyesight was jeopardized. Blurs of light and darkness filled his gaze. Footsteps sounded to his right. The Golden Bandit was getting away! Ian leaped to his feet and ran after him, barely able to see the contours of his own hallway. Chilly air wafted down the hallway in front of him. A window was open. He reached the end of the hall and looked out. A figure was trying to run through the snow. The Golden Bandit was *not* getting away this time. Ian signaled Aurora to jump.

Majestically his partner leaped through the window in a single bound, knocking the figure off his feet and into the snow as her paws struck his back. Ian was through the window before the perp could shake her off. He pinned the man down.

"Ian," the man said, his voice both familiar and muffled. "Wait!"

"You are under arrest for robbery, murder, attempted kidnapping and uttering threats," Ian said. He pulled the man's hands back firmly and handcuffed him. "You have the right to remain silent. Anything you may say could be used against you in a court of law."

"Listen!" the man said. "Son!"

Ian leaped off and flipped him over. Light sprung on from the house and behind him, cascading down from the window behind him and encircling the trees around him.

"Dad?" He looked down at his startled father. Blood trickled down his dad's face and splattered on his dress shirt and tie. Ian quickly took off the handcuffs. "Are you okay?"

"I'm fine," his father said. "It's just a nose-bleed."

"What happened? What are you doing outside?"

"I don't know," the older man said. "I was in the hallway and then someone rushed me. He elbowed me in the face and pushed out the window."

"And where is he now?"

"I d-don't know," his dad stammered again. "He ran into the trees."

A car engine sounded. Headlights disappeared through the trees. Aurora whimpered. Ian looked down and saw she was holding something in her mouth. It was the bag of stolen jewelry.

EIGHT

Ian and his father started around to the front of the house. Another car engine sounded, then a second and a third. Seemed like people were streaming from the party, hopping into their vehicles and getting out of there. And while he couldn't blame them for escaping danger, especially as they had no idea if the armed criminal was still in the house, he wished he'd managed to secure the premises and keep witnesses from leaving.

"Don't take your shirt off or clean yourself up until the crime scene investigators have seen you and given you the okay," Ian said. "It's possible the Golden Bandit got some of your blood on him when he gave you a bloody nose or you might've gotten some of his DNA on you. Either way, we might be able use that to identify him. I'm just sorry Aurora and I weren't able to stop him."

The snow was up to their knees and although his dad insisted he was fine and not injured, he was still walking slowly. As they reached the front of the house, Ian could already hear the sirens of law enforcement vehicles approaching and see the red and blue lights swirling through the trees. Then he saw Poppy leap out of her vehicle with Stormy by her side and Lorenza step out of her car. He made sure his dad was all right on his own, then ran to brief them and turn over the bag of stolen jewelry that Aurora had retrieved.

His heart pounded to get back into the house and find Tala. But the colonel assured him that she'd spoken to Tala on the phone and that it was best that law enforcement took their statements before they spoke. Reluctantly he agreed, despite everything inside him wanting to push through the crowd, run into the house and see for himself that she was safe.

By the time he'd debriefed Lorenza on everything that had happened, including how he'd found his father with a nosebleed outside in the snow, both local law enforcement and state troopers had secured the house and begun taking statements. It seemed the Golden Bandit hadn't even broken in. He'd just walked inside and thrown the power breaker. Ian's mother had switched the power back on as soon as the bandit had fled and at least twenty different people had called the police. Ian's mind swam.

Going into a party, issuing threats, stealing

jewelry and then either intentionally or accidentally ditching it made sense *how*?

He entered the house the moment he was cleared and found Tala talking with a tall, brown-haired man in a white jumpsuit. She introduced him as Bob Flocks, head of the CSI team.

"Bob and I need to go over some details," she said, almost apologetically. "I'll come find you when I'm done. Okay?"

"Sure," he said. "I'm just glad you're okay."

Something softened in her eyes. "You, too."

Ian and Aurora went to find his parents and double-checked they were fine. Then, to his frustration, all he could do was stand back and watch as his K-9 unit colleagues did their job wrapping up the scene. Less than an hour later, investigators, his colleagues and the remaining party guests left, and he was given permission to drive Tala home. But first he made sure his parents would be okay without him. Even then he left Aurora with them as added protection.

He hadn't even realized he and Tala were driving in silence until they pulled onto the main road and the sound of Tala's voice shook him out of his haze.

"Your folks will be okay," she promised, "and once the jewelry has been processed it'll be returned to its rightful owners. The whole thing was terrifying, but there were no injuries except for your father's nosebleed, the house wasn't broken into, and none of the entrances or exits were compromised. He didn't even break a window."

Her voice was soft and comforting. But he wasn't sure he wanted comfort right now.

"The Golden Bandit walked right into my house," he said. "*My house!* Where I live with my parents, and he threatened them and their guests. And I did nothing to stop him."

"You did everything you could do," she reassured him. "Ian, none of this was your fault."

Tala bit her lower lip. Then she reached for his hand across the front of the car and linked her fingers with his. But he jerked away.

"Wasn't it?" he asked. He pulled his vehicle into her driveway and cut the engine. "I wasn't even in the house when he broke in. I was out on the balcony, distracted, with you."

"Distracted," she repeated the word back. A deep chill moved through her tone. "By me."

"Yes!" he said. Wasn't that obvious? "I was paying attention to personal stuff when I should've had my eye on the ball. I shouldn't have even been out there with you."

"Right," Tala said slowly. Her voice was so cold now it was almost frozen. "I was wondering how long it was going to take before you did this."

"Did what?"

"Second-guessed what happened between us," she choked out, "and make me listen to you talk yourself out of it."

"What are you talking about?" he asked. "Obviously, I made a mistake."

Emotions he couldn't begin to decipher glistened in her eyes. "Do you regret kissing me?"

What? Where was she getting that from? He hadn't even mentioned the kiss!

"This isn't about that—"

"Please, Ian," she whispered. "Just give it to me straight. Don't make me listen to you talk yourself around in circles. Do you regret kissing me?"

"I don't know," he said. "Maybe. It's *complicated*. I'm a trooper. I should've been paying more attention."

"You were off duty and at a party," she reminded him. "You're a trooper, I'm a forensic scientist, and our lives are always going to be complicated because we literally fight crime for a living." Then he watched as her shoulders fell. "And you've always been the kind of guy who had doubts about every single relationship you've been in. But I like who I am, and I don't want you second-guessing me. I think we can both agree what happened between us was a mistake. Good night, Ian. I'll see you in the next team meeting."

He watched as she opened the car door, stepped out and shut it so hard it slammed. Ian wanted to tell her to stop and that kissing her hadn't been a mistake but instead something he'd been wanting to do for as long as he could remember. He wanted to convince her he had no regrets and would never second-guess her again. But the words faltered on his lips.

Did he regret kissing her?

He didn't actually know. It was like his feelings were drowned out by so many doubts he could barely come up for air.

Help me, Lord. I care about Tala so much and yet I'm terrified to commit myself to her.

He watched as she pulled out her cellphone and glanced at the screen. Her face paled. She opened the door and leaned back inside the car. "Ian, you've got to go home now."

Sudden fear ran down his spine.

"What happened?" he asked. "Who was that texting you? Are my parents okay?"

"That was Bob," she said. "He wanted to give me a heads-up that your dad gave both a blood and saliva sample. They matched the unknown sample found at the pawnshop last night."

"What?" He understood the words she was saying, but they made no sense. "My dad wasn't at the pawnshop last night. He was hiking alone. He does that sometimes."

"Does he have an alibi to prove that?" she asked quietly. He shook his head. She sat back down on the edge of the seat but left her legs and feet out in the snow. "You found him outside in the snow tonight with the stolen jewelry and a weird story. And now his DNA matches the unknown sample at the pawnshop."

"Well, your lab must've made a mistake," he bit out, "or the Golden Bandit got his DNA on my father to frame him—"

But when she grabbed his hand and squeezed it, he faltered.

"Ian," she said urgently. "Listen, I tested the pawnshop sample myself and was there when Bob took his DNA tonight. He tested the blood on your dad's shirt against samples of both your dad's own fresh blood and saliva samples. There's no way the crime lab would be fooled into thinking some trace DNA sample on your dad was his without checking it thoroughly. I can't explain why his DNA matches, because I don't understand it, either. But what I'm telling you is that you need to hurry up and go home. Because law enforcement will be on their way to arrest your father as the Golden Bandit."

Tala paced the living room after Ian left. Her own heartbeat was so loud she could barely hear herself think. She'd kissed Ian McCaffrey and couldn't begin to process the number of feelings that it stirred up inside her. Did she regret it? No. She cared about this man, she was attracted to him in so many ways, and she'd been brave enough to step up and let him know it—twice. And both times he'd let her down and shown her that he wasn't ready for a relationship with her. So that was that and she'd never kiss him again.

And yet, Lord, everything inside me still feels driven to help Ian, but I don't know how. Help me. Guide me. Give me wisdom.

Ian's father had been arrested on charges of being the Golden Bandit, based on evidence her lab had turned up. If law enforcement had nabbed the right man, then the case was solved, but her childhood best friend would be emotionally devastated.

But what if Ian's father *wasn't* the Golden Bandit after all?

Then what? Then the crime scene investigators made a major mistake? But how would that even happen? Bob might be a bit of an arrogant jerk, but he was a professional. The idea that her colleague had somehow altered the evidence was almost unthinkable. As was the idea that someone else on the team could do so without him noticing.

And without Tala noticing.

But if that had happened, she was going to find out.

She called a taxi and changed out of her party clothes and into a sweater and jeans while she waited for it to arrive. The Alaska State Crime Lab was empty when she arrived, except for the security guard on duty. She signed herself in with her key card and had to stop herself from actually jogging to her lab. An odd longing filled her heart as she glanced at the empty couch where she'd found Ian and Aurora dozing just a few hours before. The feelings she'd had for Ian back when they were in high school were nothing compared to the deep respect and admiration she had for him now. She might not know if Ian's father was the Golden Bandit or if Bob had altered evidence. But the one thing she did know was how to do her job. She opened the fridge.

Tala started by rechecking every piece of evidence from the crime scenes. The third and unknown blood sample found at the pawnshop was so plentiful there was no way it could be dismissed as trace. It was also fresher than the other two samples, and so was less likely to be cross-contaminated. It matched both the blood and saliva she'd watched Bob take from Ian's father. Had her colleague switched the samples somehow with the Golden Bandit's? But when? And how? And what would his motive be?

She sighed and ran her hands through her hair. That kind of speculation was the job of investigators. Her job was to focus on the facts. She went back to the evidence fridge in the hopes of finding anything she'd missed. Anything at all. Then her fingers touched a small plastic baggie containing the single spruce needle she'd found at the pawnshop. She pulled it out and dropped it on a slide and looked at it under the microscope. Huh, something was off about the shape.

She picked it up and tried to roll it between her fingers. It was flat.

She grabbed her cell and called Lorenza, even before she'd finalized her thoughts. The head of the K-9 unit answered on the first ring. "Lorenza Gallo."

"Lorenza, hi, it's Tala." She spoke so fast her words almost tripped over each other in their speed to get out. "I found a coniferous tree needle at the pawnshop crime scene in a footprint that matched the tread of the man who'd attacked me in the parking lot. So I assumed he'd tracked it in on his foot. But when I tested it in the lab, it turned out to be a *fir tree* needle, not a spruce needle. See, fir tree needles are flat, but spruce tree needles are round. The easiest way to tell them apart is to just roll them between your fingers."

"Okay..." Lorenza said. Tala could tell she didn't get it.

"There might be over a hundred and twenty million acres of forested land in Alaska," she went on to explain. "But there are only about half a dozen native species of trees—and none of them are fir. Balsam fir trees aren't native to Alaska, but they are the most popular type of Christmas tree in United States because of how full, thick and beautiful they are. Which means that tree probably didn't come from the forest. It came from someone's home!"

Lorenza let out a long breath.

"That narrows our search radius dramatically," Lorenza said. Tala could hear palpable relief coursing through the colonel's voice. The sound of a keyboard clicking came down the line. "By the look of things they're not cheap and not available from that many places. I'll get our investigators to contact local garden centers, check their staff and delivery people, and get a list of their fir tree customers. Well done, Tala. This is a solid lead. Did you happen to notice Ian's family Christmas tree?"

"It was spruce, not fir," Tala said.

"Which isn't conclusive," Lorenza said. "But a lead. Thank you. I'll keep you posted."

"Thank *you*," Tala said.

She ended the call with Lorenza and reached for it. Hope filled her heart for the first time since the investigation into the Golden Bandit had begun. Tala went back to analyzing the evidence, going over every little thing that had been collected and praying for a breakthrough.

Over an hour had passed before she next looked up to check the clock. She heard the sound of footsteps coming down the hallway and turned, wondering who else would be visiting the lab this late and hoping it was Ian.

She blinked. It was Coach Charlie.

"Hey, Tala." A grin crossed her former teacher's face. He'd changed out of the suit he'd worn at the party into blue jeans and a football jacket. "I hope you don't mind my popping in this late. Your colleague Bob told me it was okay if I brought evidence by."

"And security just buzzed you in?" she asked.

Charlie laughed self-consciously. "Oh, Bob told him to let me in. Bob's an old friend. I used to coach his kid."

Really? She thought Charlie had only coached the boy's team and Bob had daughters. Either way, it still didn't mean he should bend the rules. She called the front desk and didn't get a response, which might just mean he was on rounds. Then she sent Bob a quick question asking if he had indeed told Charlie he could drop evidence by. Bob responded immediately that he had and told security to expect him.

All right, then.

Charlie reached into his pocket and pulled out a small nugget of gold. "Can you verify what karat gold this is for me?"

"Sure. But can I ask why?"

"Maybe I'm just being an overprotective parent," he told her. "But like I told you at the party, I suspect my daughter's late husband was up to something that might possibly be connected to the Golden Bandit. But before I go to the police I'd like to see if I'm right. I trust you to be discreet."

"Okay," she said. Not that he needed a forensic scientist to check the quality of a gold nugget. Any jewelry store or pawnshop could do that much for him. Then again, they might also gossip about what they found. Not to mention she was curious. She rolled the nugget around in her fingers. By weight she'd have guessed it was about eighteen karats but when she pressed lightly with her fingertips it was as soft as twenty-four. *Odd.* She got a piece of dark black jasper stone and rubbed the gold nugget against it. Then she set the jasper inside a sample dish, got out several bottles of nitric acid of different concentrations and, starting with the weakest dilutions, tested it on the jasper. The gold remnant didn't fade.

"Where did she find this nugget?" she asked.

"In an old abandoned mine."

"Well, it's twenty-four karat," she said. "That means it's a hundred percent gold with no impurities."

Relief flickered in his eyes. "That's a good thing, right?"

"Actually, no," she replied. "Most gold nuggets found in the Alaskan wild are only twenty karats. A few are as much as twenty-two. Not completely pure gold without impurities. Also, the weight seems off. Do you mind if I try to break this open?"

Charlie's eyebrows quirked. "Go ahead."

If need be she had multiple tools in the lab that used lasers to measure density, for purposes like dating bones to calculate the age of a victim. But she preferred simpler options when possible. She set the gold nugget on the table and used a small chisel and hammer to break it open. Sure enough, there was a much harder nugget of gold hidden inside the softer layer, like a chocolate-covered peanut. She repeated the jasper process again with the harder inner nugget. This time the sample reacted instantly to the first solution.

"I'm sorry, but it's only nine karats," she said. "It's definitely not a real nugget found in a mine. If I was to venture a guess, someone melted down cheap gold, formed a nugget and then dipped it in a thick layer of expensive gold." She furrowed her brow. "It's a pretty clever crime. The average person wouldn't think to check for multiple layers and the average pawnshop outside Alaska would just quote it at whatever their standard price for junk gold is, melt it down with a larger batch and never know the difference. A lot of pawnshops tend to be pretty diplomatic about pretending grandma's ring is twenty-four karat when it's only eighteen."

But a smart pawnshop or jeweler in Alaska would know the difference. And why would he think this linked to the Golden Bandit? Did Charlie think the killer had been stealing gold to melt into nuggets? Or that someone working at an Alaska pawnshop received one of these fake nuggets from a customer and figured out what was happening, so the Golden Bandit was created to cover his tracks?

"If someone wanted to make a more authentic-looking gold nugget," Charlie said, "one that fooled people like you, how would they do it?"

"You can't fool people like me," she said. "It's a smart crime, but not a foolproof one. And I'm still not about to help anyone cheat."

He laughed. "What does that mean? You think my daughter or I are making fake nuggets? Maybe hiding them in mines for gullible tourists to find?"

Suspicion dripped down her spine. She had absolutely no doubt Charlie would try to cover for his daughter like he'd covered for the bullies on his hockey team? She reached for her phone and started typing a text to Ian.

Charlie's in lab with fake nugget—

"Drop the phone, now!"

Charlie reached into his jacket and pulled out a handgun.

She hit Send without finishing the text, hoping he wouldn't notice, and let the phone clatter and fall. Fear washed over her. Prayers for help and rescue filled her heart.

"To be fair, I didn't expect to convince you." Charlie aimed the weapon between her eyes. "But

I was hoping you'd pass my gold nugget test and I wouldn't have to hurt you. I mean, how much trouble can one dorky little scientist be? Half an hour ago, I got a phone call from my friend at a garden center warning me that cops might be coming around to check out my *Christmas tree* because some nosy little person at a science lab might've found a needle from my tree at a crime scene. Seriously, Tala, coming after my Christmas tree now? I don't like the idea of killing a former student, Tala. But you've given me no choice."

NINE

Ian paced back and forth in the hallway in the Anchorage police station with a puzzled but loyal Aurora one step behind him, until an older officer finally called him and told him he could see his father.

"We're keeping him overnight," the officer said professionally but not unkindly. "Hopefully he'll be able to be seen by a judge before Christmas and he'll set bail."

Ian hoped so. The police station had such bad cell service he hadn't been able to check his texts or call around for a lawyer. But how would they find money for bail? Let alone even afford an attorney? He thanked the officer who escorted him into an interview room, where he found his father sitting at a table in handcuffs, looking ten years older than earlier that evening.

"Hey, Dad," Ian said softly. He sat down in the chair opposite his father, wishing he could give him a hug. "How are you doing?"

"I can't complain," his dad responded. "Everyone's just doing their job. I just wish I knew how my blood ended up at a crime scene. I did donate blood at the high school hockey blood drive a few weeks ago. Maybe someone stole that blood and placed it there."

Tala had said that the Golden Bandit had smelled like blood.

"We'll look into it," Ian assured him. "If anyone can figure that out, it's Tala." A sad sigh moved through him as he remembered how he'd left things with her. Aurora laid her head on Ian's knee and he gently stroked her soft fur. "I just wish I'd been partnered with a search and rescue dog or one who specialized in pursuit, and we'd been able to stop him from getting away."

"You'd better stop that kind of talk," his dad said, "before you owe her an apology."

"Tala?" Ian asked. How did his dad know about that?

"No, son." His dad managed a half-hearted chuckle. "I mean your loyal partner here, Aurora. You prayed so long and hard to be partnered with a cadaver dog. And when that happened you barely stopped to thank God before rushing into wondering whether you would've been better off with a different type of dog. Aurora's amazing and she obviously loves being your K-9 partner. Stop letting your low self-esteem get in the way of that and trust you're paired with her for a reason."

Ian sat back with a grimace. He'd come here to comfort his dad, and here he was getting a fatherly lecture!

"Grandma always said that McCaffrey men have foolish hearts," Ian said.

"Yeah, she did," his dad concurred. "Because your grandfather was a very loving man who was a complete fool when it came to finances. You're not him and I'd like to think we've both learned from his mistakes. You have a wonderful career and an amazing woman by your side in Tala."

Ian swallowed hard.

"I've made some serious mistakes with Tala," he admitted.

"We all do," the older man said. "The only thing that matters is if you've apologized and there's a way to make things right."

He was about to tell his dad that he and Tala weren't really a couple, when the memory of the way it had felt to hold her in his arms filled his mind. Who was he kidding? Ian had romantic feelings for her and more. He always had. He'd just been too worried about messing it up to do anything about it. Ian and his dad made small talk for a while before an officer knocked on the door and let Ian know it was time to go. As he and Aurora said goodbye to his dad and headed down the hall there was no doubt in his mind where he was going next. He had to find Tala and apologize.

Lord, please forgive me for complaining about Aurora as much as I do and for doubting the desires and drives You've placed on my heart. Help me trust my own heart and the person You've called me to be.

He reached the front door and bent down to give Aurora a scratch. She licked his fingers and he knew all was forgiven. His phone pinged as missed text messages rushed in. He glanced at them and felt his face pale. What was Charlie doing at Tala's lab after hours? He tried Tala's phone and it went to voice mail. His heart stuttering in his chest, Ian drove as fast as he dared to the lab and found the parking lot empty except for the security guard's truck and a nondescript van. Even before he'd pulled to a stop, he heard Aurora bark sharply. His partner was sitting at attention on the passenger seat.

"Aurora, what's wrong?"

She barked again, urgently and in a higher pitch this time. Her ears perked and her nose strained toward the van, warning and alerting him that something was wrong. He opened his door and had barely stepped out when she leaped through the door after him. Her paws danced in the snow impatiently as he clipped on her leash.

"Okay, I hear you," he said. "Show me."

She pulled him across the parking lot toward

the van. Was there a corpse inside the vehicle? The engine roared and its headlights flashed. Then the vehicle screeched out of the parking lot. Ian glanced at the building. There was no security guard sitting at the front desk. Aurora howled in the direction of the departing van. He'd never seen her more insistent.

"Yeah, I got it," he told his partner. "We won't let the van get away."

He ran back to his vehicle, calling the situation in to law enforcement as he went. Aurora jumped in and they peeled out onto the road. The van's taillights flickered ahead of him. Spurred on by Aurora's urgent barks, he chased after it, praying for the safety of whoever might be in danger inside. He pursued it deeper and deeper into the woods, watching as the taillights disappeared and reappeared through the trees ahead of him. Until finally he hit a fork in the road. Snow-covered roads spread off in either side, with any tire tracks wiped away by the wind and snow. For a long and agonizing moment, he stared into the darkness. He couldn't see the headlights anywhere. Then he groaned in frustration. He'd lost it.

Aurora barked.

"I don't know where he's gone!" Ian argued back.

His partner barked again. Seemed she wasn't taking no for an answer. He knew cadaver dogs could smell a long distance, but could she track the van? It was worth a shot. He rolled both windows down.

"Which way?" he asked Aurora. "Show me!"

She practically leaped over him, her feet landing on his lap as she stuck her head out of his widow and barked.

"Got it." He nudged her back into the passenger seat and kept driving. Moments later he saw the van parked off the road half-hidden in the trees. Ian and Aurora ran for it. The van's front seat was empty. He yanked the back door open. There was nothing but an empty blanket inside, but Aurora's reaction left him no doubt that she'd detected the scent of death on it. There'd been a corpse in this van.

Ian whispered a prayer and then radioed in his location and what he'd found. His phone buzzed with a text from Sean, telling him that officers had already convened on both the lab and Tala's home. She was nowhere to be found.

His legs faltered and he sank to his knees in the snow.

Lord, please help me find Tala. I need to know she's safe.

Then he heard a distant scream pierce the air. He looked down at Aurora.

"I need your help," he said. "Your senses are better than mine. Help me find Tala!"

He tightened his hand around Aurora's leash, and they ran toward the sound, side by side. He could feel Aurora urging him on, guiding him with little tugs on the leash, just as he guided her. Then the trees parted, and he saw Tala fighting for her life as Charlie yanked her at gunpoint toward an abandoned mine.

"Ian!" she called. "Charlie's the Golden Bandit!"

"Let her go!" Ian shouted. *"Now!"*

Aurora barked, and Ian knew somehow she was telling him to let her go. He dropped the leash. The German shepherd snarled, her teeth flashing as she sprang toward Charlie. Charlie let go of Tala and fired at the dog. Tala spun hard, raised her fist and punched Charlie in the jaw, sending him sprawling, just as Aurora landed on top of him, pinning him with her paws.

"You're under arrest!" Ian snarled. He stood over his former hockey coach and kicked the gun from his hands. "For kidnapping, murder and theft."

He wasn't about to use a cutesy nickname for the man's crimes and hoped the moniker Golden Bandit would disappear from history. Ian signaled to Aurora to step back. She did so, and he grabbed Charlie's hands and cuffed them.

Then Ian left him there, stood up and reached for Tala. He pulled her into his arms.

"He kidnapped me from the lab," she said breathlessly. "His daughter's mining business was a fraud. Either one of them, or both of them, was melting down jewelry and pretending they were raw nuggets."

"He was also involved in a blood drive my dad donated to," Ian told her. "I'm guessing that's how he faked the crime scene."

"Then he might've staged that robbery at your house to frame him," she said.

Sirens sounded in the distance and lights flashed through the trees. Backup was coming. He wrapped his arms around her and pulled her closer into his arms.

"I'm sorry I wasn't here earlier," he rasped, "and for everything I said."

"It's okay," she said. "I can't believe Aurora was able to track me."

Just then Aurora whined urgently. He looked down at his partner. Her ears were still perked, her feet danced in the snow and her nose strained toward the abandoned mine.

"I'm not sure she was only tracking you," he said, easing Tala out of his arms. Officers ran toward them in the snow. He informed them that Charlie was under arrest and borrowed a flashlight from an Anchorage officer. Then he allowed Aurora to guide him to the mine, with Tala by his side. They climbed down a snowy slope, reached the mine and walked through the labyrinth of tunnels following Aurora's lead.

She reached an empty space and barked at the floor, the sound echoing around them on all sides.

He knelt down, pulled loose rocks away, then shone his light down toward the hole and felt a prayer of thanksgiving pass his lips.

It looked like they'd found the bodies of the missing pawn workers.

The morning sky was a dark purple with just slivers of gold and pink on the horizon when Tala came down the stairs to her living room and searched for her cell phone to call a taxi to take her to work.

It had been a late night. Charlie and his daughter had both been arrested and five sets of human remains in total had been found hidden in the abandoned mine, including Millie's ex-husband and the Alaska State Crime Lab's security guard, who Charlie had killed and quickly dumped in the mine earlier that night while Tala was still analyzing evidence upstairs. A search of Millie's home had turned up clean, but Charlie's had apparently turned up reams of stolen jewelry and the equipment he'd used to melt it into nuggets, along with a partially empty bag of Ian's father's blood. State troopers, Anchorage officers and crime scene investigators had worked together well into the night to collect evidence and process multiple locations. Eventually an officer had driven her home, long after midnight, and she'd fallen into a deep and dreamless sleep.

While she'd lost sight of Ian in the crowd

shortly after Aurora had found the bodies, somehow the brief hug they'd shared when he'd run to her rescue had spoken volumes. God had brought Ian back into her life—stronger and better than she'd ever imagined, tugging on her heartstrings and making her feel things she didn't know how to put into words.

But what happened now?

Headlights cast a gentle glow on her living room curtains. Moments later she heard an SUV door close and footprints crunching on the snow outside.

She slid the curtains back to see Ian and Aurora sitting side by side on the top step of her porch, just where he used to sit waiting for her when they were younger. She opened the door and they both leaped to their feet.

"Good morning," she said.

"Hey!" A goofy, almost shy grin crossed his face, reminding her of both the boy she'd cared about so much when they were young and the amazing man she was discovering now. He held up a tray of coffees and a paper bag. "I got breakfast to go and wondered if you wanted a ride to work."

"Thank you," she said. "There's a lot of evidence from yesterday to process and I want to get right on it."

He chuckled. "I knew you would."

She thanked God the crime had been closed

and prayed for the family and friends of the security guard and those who were processing the news that their loved ones' bodies had been found. Now it was time to get to work analyzing the evidence to ensure his former coach aka the Golden Bandit would be going to prison for a very long time.

Ian took Aurora and the food to his vehicle and she ducked back into the house to get her bag together and put on her coat and boots. When she opened the door again, Ian was standing alone on the porch and Aurora's tail was wagging happily at her from the front seat of the car.

"You trust her alone in there with our breakfast?" she asked.

"She's a state trooper," he said, "and also knows there's a sausage in it for her if she's patient."

Tala laughed and stepped outside to join Ian on the porch. He took both of her gloved hands in his and looked down at their linked fingers.

"There's a K-9 unit Christmas party coming up," he said. "I know you're used to mostly seeing the team through a screen, but I'd like it if you came with me, as my date. Also, my parents want to invite you to our home for Christmas dinner. They adore you and want to make their next charity drive for the hospice your grandmother passed in." Then he looked up into her eyes. "I just want you to be part of my life, Tala, this Christmas and always."

She searched his gaze and felt something deep and beyond words well up in her heart. "I'd like that, very much."

Was he saying what she hoped he was?

"I've presumed you knew how I felt for far too long when I should've just come out and said it," he said gruffly. "You're the best friend I've ever had and the most beautiful woman I've ever seen. You impress me every day with your drive and your heart. You're the only person I've ever imagined spending my life with."

I love you, Ian, and I have for so long. The words filled her heart but something stopped her lips from saying it.

"Turns out there was a reward for finding the ring that Aurora and I dropped off at the mall the other day," he said. "It wasn't huge, but it was enough for me to get you something."

He dropped her hands, reached into his pocket and pulled out a ring box. He opened it. A delicate band of woven yellow and white gold lay inside. Ian knelt on one knee.

"This is my promise to you that one day you'll be my wife," he said, "and that no matter the doubts I have about me or how I second-guess myself, I will always love you, be true to you and come home to you. Will you marry me and be mine, Tala? This Christmas and forever?"

A sob choked in her throat. "I love you, too, Ian. I always have."

Hope filled his gaze. "Is that a yes?"

"Yes!" Tears and laughter mingled on her lips as he gently pulled her glove off and slipped the ring onto her finger. "I'll marry you and spend the rest of my life with you."

Then Ian leaped to his feet and pulled her into his chest. "I'll get you a better engagement ring when I can."

"This is perfect," she said. "This is all I need."

Because it was Ian and they were together, and he'd promised that no matter what, he'd always love her. She kissed his lips, he kissed her back, and she knew the man she'd waited her whole life for would be by her side forever.

* * * * *

Dear Reader,

This is the third K-9 Christmas novella I've written and I absolutely love the joy they bring to my holidays. I hope you've gotten as much happiness out of the stories about Aurora, Liberty and Garfunkel that I have.

It's been a different Christmas for me this year because I wasn't able to see friends I usually celebrate with. The amazing owner of the salon I go to is running a gift-giving drive for seniors in our community who do not have families. I've also been chatting online with a reader who's spending her Christmas alone in the hospital.

My prayer is that whatever Christmas holds for you this year, you'll be surrounded by people who care for you, and find the peace and joy of knowing you are loved and have a purpose.

Thank you, as always, for your letters and messages. I really love receiving them. As always you can reach me on facebook and twitter at @maggiekblack or email me through my website at maggiekblack.com.

Merry Christmas and thank you for sharing this journey with me,

Mags

ALASKAN CHRISTMAS CHASE

Lenora Worth

Dedicated to the people of Alaska,
and the amazing history of that beautiful land.

Yea, the darkness hideth not from thee;
but the night shineth as the day: the darkness
and the light are both alike to thee.
— *Psalms* 139:12

ONE

Besides working with the Alaska K-9 Unit, the only thing Eli Partridge and Mallory Haru had in common was that they both wore glasses and worked more than they socialized.

Which was why Eli had been willing when Colonel Lorenza Gallo had suggested he help Mallory, a criminal psychologist, with a K-9 she'd worked to rehabilitate. Koko, a big lovable Malinois, had been injured and traumatized a few months ago while on a drug bust deep in the Alaskan wilderness area near Girdwood. His human partner had taken a job in California after he was released from the hospital, so that left Koko without a handler. But he'd get a new partner once he was clear for law enforcement again.

"I'm so excited, Eli," Mallory had told him two days ago, when he'd asked her about Koko and suggested she bring the dog here where it was quiet and off the beaten path. "I work with human members on the team, but I also love helping traumatized dogs. I begged Colonel Lorenza to let me work with Koko. He needs to find his confidence and go back to being a good K-9, and that means more therapy—the kind I can give him. But I need your input."

How could he refuse the woman he'd had a little bit of a crush on since the first day he'd met her? Mallory was gorgeous, divorced and about four years older than Eli. They worked closely together at times, and sometimes they didn't always agree, but tonight would be the first time Mallory had ever reached out to him in a personal way.

"It's not a date," he told himself as he roamed the small cabin he'd bought a couple of years ago. His place backed up to the Chugach State Park, where he liked to hike and camp out whenever he had time off.

Fluffing pillows and making sure the floors were clean and his gym clothes had been washed and put away, he checked the roaring fire, then glanced out the window. A December snowstorm had created a near whiteout, but Mallory was born in Alaska. She knew these back roads better than most. Her sturdy Jeep would have no problem making the trip across town.

Eli stirred the chili he'd prepared and opened the fridge to make sure the cheese dip would be firm. Then he looked at the white spruce he'd cut down this afternoon and hurriedly decorated with his nerdy comic book hero ornaments along with the obligatory lights and other Christmas baubles. He'd placed the tiny angel ornament his godmother had given him last Christmas on the top of the four-foot-high tree.

"Thank you, Bettina. You know how much this angel ornament means to me," he whispered, remembering the good times they'd had.

Her house was just around the bend from this cabin. He'd been watching it while she'd been battling cancer.

Bettina had told him to get on with his life. *I know you're afraid of marriage after witnessing your parents go at each other, but one day you'll find a woman who appreciates you and loves you*, she had advised. *When you're ready, you'll find her.*

Bettina was in hospice and had almost died, but she'd had a turnaround the doctors called miraculous and was holding her own for now.

He wasn't sure he'd ever be ready for a wife and family. But he was ready to get to know Mallory away from work. Still, what if he messed things up? What if he made things awkward like he'd done in high school and college? Then he'd lose her as a friend. While they worked in different parts of the building, him being a tech expert and her being a psychologist, they ran into each other when dealing with certain cases. He always enjoyed their talks—okay, arguments and heavy discussions—whether about work or his

Transformers collection. He liked being around Mallory. He just wasn't sure he'd ever be able to take the next step with anyone, not after the mess of a marriage his parents had back in Oregon. When he heard a motor shutting down outside, he headed to the window. Mallory's black Jeep hulked in the snow like a robotic creature ready to pounce. He watched as she coaxed Koko out of the kennel. The big dog hurled down onto the packed snow and barked.

"I don't blame you, boy," Eli said, opening the door. "Hi, Mallory." Koko still got that sad look in his eyes at times, but Mallory had helped with his trauma.

Mallory glanced behind her and then hurried up to the porch, her black puffer coat covering her from her neck to her knees where bright blue snow boots took over. Before Eli could say another word, she grabbed his hand and tugged him inside.

Then she slammed the door and whirled to stare at him, panic glimmering in her beautiful brown eyes. "Someone was following me, Eli. They tried to run me off the road."

Eli checked her over while alarms sounded inside his head. "Are you all right?"

"I'm fine," she said. Then she commanded the dog to sit. "Koko barked warnings. That's all well and good, but I had to keep driving. He sensed something was off. That's at least progress on his recovery."

So like Mallory to focus on her patient's needs, instead of worrying about almost being driven into a snowbank by another vehicle.

She bent to pet the furry dog. "You're a good boy, Koko. I believe you've still got what it takes."

Eli kneeled to praise the dog, knowing how important praise and play toys were in getting the K-9 back into action. "Way to go, Koko."

Koko's eyes widened and his ears perked up.

Eli's radar perked up, too. Who would want to harm Mallory? Giving her a once-over, he asked, "Are you sure you're okay?"

"I'm shaken, but better now. I guess I'm being paranoid," she said. "My ex-husband and I aren't exactly friendly, and it would be so like him to get drunk and try to mess with me."

Being so close to Mallory made Eli even more nervous than the fidgety dog between them. Her inky, chin-length, chunky hair and her dark eyes contrasted with her pale, glowing complexion. He smiled at her and she smiled back. She wore a pure red lipstick that gave her street cred for sure.

He needed to get it together. The howling wind and falling snow had him listening for the dings and crashes coming from outside. "Tell me more about this vehicle that bumped you. Could the driver have lost control?"

"The first time, yes," she said, her expression

somber now. "But by the third bump, I decided he was after me."

"*He?* You saw the driver?"

"It was hard to see, so I can't be sure. I don't know what I did to provoke this."

Before he could respond, a gunshot rang out and a nearby window shattered, sending glass shards across the room like falling icicles. Without thinking, he shoved Mallory down and covered her with his body.

Koko barked at the door, growling and pawing. The big boy still had trouble following commands, but he was good at barking warnings.

Eli glanced down at Mallory. Her eyes were wide, her pupils dilated, her breathing fast. "He must have followed me here."

Eli had to register what had just happened, while he savored holding her in his arms. "You weren't kidding, were you?"

TWO

Mallory pushed at her bangs and made sure her glasses still worked. "I never kid about such things."

Why did every relationship she tried to develop always go oh-so-wrong? Well, this wasn't really a new relationship, because she only needed Eli's observations and opinion. They worked together and he was available and knowledgeable. The tech guru was great with the K-9s, and Koko needed every bit of praise and reentry training he could get.

She'd agreed to collaborate with Eli after Colonel Gallo had suggested this meeting. Besides, Mallory was conscious of the chemistry that seemed to sizzle whenever she and Eli were together, and she saw this as a way to break the awkwardness caused by that awareness. A sensation she'd tried to ignore because she liked Eli—as a friend. Nothing more could happen between them. She'd worked too hard to get over her ex-husband to turn around and fall for a coworker. She'd married Ned in haste and regretted it almost immediately. Never again would she let another person make her doubt herself or her work.

Bottom line? Eli was great as a coworker and friend, and she wanted to keep it that way. But being tapped by a massive truck on an icy road and then getting shot at, *not* so great.

Eli motioned for her to scoot over toward the kitchen counter where they'd be safe behind the wide, thick structure. "We need to stay away from windows."

"I didn't bring a gun." She knew that sounded silly. "I have a permit and I've been through training, but I rarely carry my official weapon."

Eli crawled to a cabinet and opened a drawer. "I have one right here. I don't carry it much, either, but I did train with the K-9 handlers when I first came here. I wanted to understand things better. They worked with me on weaponry. I can shoot when I need to. Only, I've never needed to—yet."

Eli was like her—studious and more of a nerd than an officer of the law. But they'd both worked hard to be a part of the K-9 unit. She didn't want to be put to the test like this, on a snowy December night when they were all alone with an unknown assailant and a K-9 in need of a lot of TLC.

"Have you ever been shot at before?" she asked, thankful the shooter had missed them.

"No," he admitted, that shyness she liked coming over his face. "You?"

She shook her head. "Who would do this?"

"You mentioned your ex?"

"He did carry. He had all sorts of guns—both legal and illegal—it turns out. One of the many reasons I left him."

"Do you think he could be out there? Is he the jealous type?"

"Yes, and yes." She couldn't lie. Ned had turned out to be a big disappointment. An outdoorsman who took things to extremes and only wanted to discuss guns and conspiracy theories instead of marriage and commitments. "But... I heard he moved to Juneau to work on a trail crew."

"Good to know," Eli said as he checked his weapon and loaded the fifteen-round magazine into the semiautomatic pistol. He scooted back toward her and then looked at her, his dark blue eyes full of an earnest light that had always drawn her to him. Not how she wanted their first away-from-work-but-still-work evening to go. But then, Eli didn't have a clue about her or her feelings, and technically, this was truly work-related.

A crash sounded outside, causing Koko to go wild, barking and snarling at the door.

"Koko acts as if he's picked up a familiar scent," she said, wondering if the dog recognized the person outside, and trying not to panic. But her heart raced, all the same.

Then another noise pierced the air, like glass breaking out farther away from the house.

"What was that?" she asked Eli, her pulse trying to catch up with her heart. Even though they worked in a dangerous profession, she'd never felt threatened like this before.

Eli whispered, "Could be the wind, or we have someone snooping around. I'm guessing it's not the wind. I'm going out back to see who it is."

"Is that a good idea?"

She didn't want him to go out in the storm and get shot. Koko might be of some help, but it was too soon to see if her many hours of therapy with the dog had accomplished anything.

"You have a better idea?" he asked. Then he sniffed. "The chili I made is probably scorching right now."

He'd made chili. She loved chili. He knew that because they'd talked about it last week.

"No, I don't have any ideas," she replied to his question. "Maybe I cut them off when I almost missed the turn, and now they want to retaliate?"

"I have to check it out," he said. "This place is so isolated—one reason I keep a weapon close."

"So, what's your plan?" she asked now, training overtaking fear. "I was almost run down, someone shot through the window and we keep hearing things. I think we're in trouble."

"I'm fully aware of that," he replied. "Which is why I have to go and check outside."

"Then I'm going with you," she said. "Koko can at least sniff and bark."

"Are you sure Koko is ready for this?"

"Part of the therapy and training," she answered. "He's improved so much over the last few weeks. The team trusts me with him—as a temporary handler—because they've tried all the right stuff. He runs through his paces with flying colors, but emotionally, he needs someone like me to understand him."

If only she could understand her own wayward emotions. They could be in deep trouble, but regardless, she felt safe with Eli.

"Okay, we'll take him with us—to warn us—if nothing else. He's got his official vest on, so that's good."

Koko's dark eyes brightened, and his ears perked up. "See, he knows we're discussing him," she said. "Koko, we need you."

The Malinois danced around her, thinking it was playtime. He lived for his chew toy and didn't realize it was part of his training. "I think he's in agreement on that."

Eli's doubtful expression didn't give her much hope. His frown was adorable, but also determined. Pushing at his thick, shaggy hair, he said, "You two stay with me, understand?"

"Yessir," she said with a mock salute, trying to be brave. "You're bossy."

"No, I'm *concerned*. Someone followed you here and then shot at us, so we're in trouble. Especially if they're still snooping around."

Mallory took a deep breath, hoping she could stop shaking. "You're right. We should call for backup."

"Not yet," he said. "I'm trained and I have good reflexes."

"Right." She looked him over. He was in good shape. She'd seen him in the workout room, and she'd felt his biceps when he'd gallantly pushed her to the floor and protected her. But he didn't have much street action. Neither did she. "But we still need backup."

"You don't trust me?"

"I don't want you to get hurt."

His eyes, so deep blue and questioning, moved over her face.

"So we'll go together, and hope Koko can alert and maybe attack if needed, right?"

"Right. This will be a good time to prove himself. A good plan." She hoped. "Meantime, I'll call for backup."

"Okay, are you ready?"

She nodded and made the call. Then she saw a hockey stick by the other door. "I'll use this as my weapon."

He winced. "Don't break my hockey stick, okay?"

"Only if I have to protect you or Koko with it."

Giving her an appreciative glance, Eli went over the plan. "We'll walk the perimeters of the property and stay in the shadows. If you have a hat in your tote bag, get it now."

"I have a hat and gloves," she said, crawling to where she'd dropped her bag by the door, careful to avoid the glass by the window. Soon she was covered from head to toe. Maybe all that bundling would protect her from a bullet.

As they crawled toward the back door, Eli managed to reach up and find the stove knob to turn off the chili.

"We'll have dinner later," he said, but he didn't sound too confident.

Eli stayed in front of Mallory and Koko. She'd given the dog the quiet command, and so far, he was obeying. Eli prayed Koko wouldn't go wild and start barking again. They probably should have left him in the house, but Mallory was right. Koko had to be tested and what better time than now, after all the excitement earlier? They had to find out what was going on.

Maybe a bad case of road rage? Or something much worse?

Eli feared the second scenario. They worked with people who took out criminals every day, so they had access to criminal records and all kinds of information that never made it to the public. Of course, criminals tended to hold grudges. What if someone could be retaliating?

He glanced around the wide backyard that sat below a jutting bluff, not far from the Chugach State Park. Eli had often hiked along these trails, so he knew the path up to that bluff. If they could get up there, they'd have a good view of the open ground between the house and the thicket. But that could be treacherous in the ice and snow.

They heard another noise. "That's coming from inside the barn," he whispered.

The small barn was about fifty yards from his cabin, toward the back of the property. It needed some work, but it was sturdy and built to last. Unless someone worked on destroying it right now.

Mallory held to the back of his jacket, Koko by her side. The dog growled low, meaning he could sense the danger. But did he know the intruder?

Mallory held on to Eli. "Why hasn't someone arrived from headquarters?"

"Snow, ice, treacherous roads," he explained. "They're short-staffed during the holidays."

"The dispatcher said she'd send someone immediately, but this place isn't easy to find even when you're in law enforcement."

Eli could agree with that. Though he liked the isolation most days. "Meantime, let's check it out."

They maneuvered their way around trees and shrubs, but when they didn't see anyone, Eli motioned to her. They slipped up onto the back porch of the barn. It sat dark and shuttered, its roofline hunched over with heavy snow.

Another crash and then someone came hurling out onto the small porch and fell at their feet. Eli went into action and jumped the man, holding him down, his gun pressing into the man's ribs. "Start talking! Who are you and why are you here?"

A shaky voice called out, "Eli, it's me. Aidan. Don't shoot me, please."

Mallory let out a held breath while Eli flipped the man over. "Who's Aidan?"

"My brother."

Eli held the gun away as he let the boy go. "Aidan, what's going on? Did you follow Mallory here? Did you run her off the road and then shoot at us?"

The boy's breath came in panting huffs. He looked scared and confused, thick bangs jutting out from his black wool cap. "Yes, I tried to get her off the road, but I wasn't the one doing the shooting. I was trying to stall her, to get her out of the way. I came here to warn you. Someone's out to kill both of us." Then he glanced at Mallory. "And probably you, too."

THREE

"Okay, Aidan, start over from the beginning," Eli said, running a hand over his shaggy bangs after Mallory handed him a cup of coffee. Still reeling from finding his brother on his property, he hadn't gotten past Aidan, a freshman in college, being in some sort of deep trouble. They were actually half-brothers, since Eli's father had a brief affair with another woman when Eli was ten years old. She'd abandoned the baby, and that left Dad to take care of Aidan. Things around their house had been tense for a while, but at least his mother loved Aidan, too.

Eli had just returned with Koko and was still in shock from finding his younger brother crashing through a barn door. He'd sent Aidan and Mallory inside once Aidan warned them that they were all in danger. Everett Brand, a local police officer now engaged and about to be married to team member Helena Maddox, had heard the call and come to the rescue. He'd managed to chase down the SUV leaving the premises. Everett had called in reinforcements to scour the woods for evidence, too.

Mallory gave him a questioning stare. "Before Aidan explains, what happened out there?"

Eli sipped his coffee and then set the cup on the counter. "Koko and I pursued the intruder into the woods on the north side of the property. We could see deep tracks in the snow, but unfortunately we lost the scent. When I heard sirens, I pulled Koko back." He brushed off his jeans and boots. "The snow out there is knee-deep. We met Everett at the road, but when Koko alerted and tugged toward the driveway, Everett and I followed. The vehicle took off as we rounded the curve, spinning out on the snow. Everett went after it, but radioed he'd lost the SUV on the main road."

Mallory lowered her head. "So this person is still on the loose."

"Yes."

Eli nodded. "I gave the colonel a detailed report. Meanwhile, we're on the lookout for the man who forced Aidan to come here."

Earlier, Aidan had given Eli a good description and the man's name, but they all figured that was an alias. He'd go to ground, but they'd keep looking. Lorenza would have someone scouring the whole of Anchorage and beyond.

The kid was shivering now, whether from the

bitter cold or fright, Eli couldn't be sure. But the warm fire and the hot coffee should help. "Aidan? We need to hear your side of this."

Mallory sat petting Koko. The K-9 had done his job by alerting and barking enough to scare away whoever was with Aidan. But his brother was right. They'd be back. Aidan knew the man who'd wanted to kill them. That wouldn't go well when he reported back to the whole gang.

Aidan gulped his coffee, then put the cup on the table beside the worn brown couch. "Lena Matson," he said. "She got me mixed up in this mess."

"Who is Lena?" Mallory asked, her eyes laser sharp as she went from concerned friend into her professional protocol.

"A girl I met at school," Aidan replied. "We hit it off kinda quick, like, she got me, or so I thought."

"Go on," Mallory said while Eli brought over bowls of slightly scorched chili.

Aidan grabbed the chili. "I'm so hungry."

"Talk and eat," Eli said. Why were teenagers *always* hungry?

Aidan shoved a spoonful of the meaty chili into his mouth, then drank the water Mallory had brought to him once they'd gotten him to the cabin.

"I met Lena in a study group," Aidan said.

"She was behind on math and history. Or so she said."

Eli glanced at Mallory, thinking this could take all night. "Aidan, speed this up. We've got to decide what to do before these people send someone else."

Aidan finished the food. "We got to know each other, but I noticed she dressed in really nice clothes, so I figured she was way out of my league. Her parents live in a big, fancy house and her dad owns some type of construction business— but that's just a cover." He shot Eli an apologetic glance. "They want your property, too."

Eli took notes. "Okay, so she has money, and her dad wants this property—*my* property? Why?"

"Yeah, that's the weird part—as a cover. They need secluded properties like this one and… I bragged on it and on you. Once I realized I'd been tricked, I thought back over the whole group. These kids come from nice families, so they don't need to go around doing snatch-and-grabs."

Eli held up his hand. "Wait, what?"

"They run a huge robbery ring," Aidan said. "I found out when Lena took me to a house that's three times the size of hers. And hers is huge."

"Why did she take you there?"

"The big man lives there. *The leader*, she called him. Her dad works for him. They wanted me to join up," he explained. "And…she'd told the man about *this* place because I went on and on to her one night about how my big brother lives here and owns a lot of acreage. Now they want it and they offered a huge price. But I told them you wouldn't sell." He shrugged. "But they looked up the info and saw the deed, Eli. They find stuff like that and use it to their advantage."

Eli glanced from Aidan to Mallory. "They can't buy something that isn't for sale."

"They can if everyone involved is dead," Aidan blurted. "I said no, we couldn't sell, and things got worse from there. Lena told me I needed to comply, or bad things would happen to the people I care about, even Mom and Dad. They want this property, Eli. They figured they'd just get you out of the way, I guess. I don't know."

"So why did one of them come here with you?" Mallory asked, her hand stroking Koko's head.

"I had to think fast," Aidan replied. "I told Lena okay, I'd see what I could do. I told them I'd talk to you. I wanted to buy myself some time."

Eli glanced at his brother, his expression grim. "So that's why you came early? It's close to Christmas break."

"Yeah, but they sent one of their lackeys to watch over me—meaning they didn't want me to come here on my own. They needed to trust me, so to speak." He leaned back on the couch, fatigue obvious as shadows played across his face. "So Frederick, the human tree—or *Tree*, as we call him—came with me, in his vehicle. He made me drive, you know, to keep me from, like, jumping from the car."

"Frederick, the man with apparently only one name and one nickname, is the man who wanted to kill us?"

"Yes, and he's also the man who tried to kill me when I ruined his sniper-perfect shot. Eli, you'd be dead right now if I hadn't done something."

Eli nodded. "I appreciate your efforts. Why did you feel the need to run Mallory off the road?"

"Because she was *on* the road," Aidan said. "The road to your house, a road that's less traveled, unless someone is purposely coming to your house. Mallory was collateral damage—in the way. They don't like witnesses, but they also don't leave any evidence. They would have made your death look like an accident, but someone else being here made things dicey—according to Tree. And, no offense, Mallory, but you were driving really slow."

Mallory glanced at the whiteout glistening from the front porch lights. "For obvious reasons."

"I understand," Aidan said. "But Tree—he gets kind of antsy about things, and he wanted you out of the way. So he grinned, held a gun to my head and ordered me to tap your SUV with his SUV, know what I mean?"

Mallory nodded. "I do. At first, I thought I'd

imagined it but after you kept coming, I got a little scared."

"I'm sorry," Aidan said, a sincerely contrite expression on his face. "I recognized your SUV from seeing it at headquarters when Eli gave me a tour, and I didn't want to hurt you. I hoped you'd pull over and let us by. But then, Tree would have shot you if you had pulled over." He held his hands in his shaggy dark hair. "I didn't know what to do."

Mallory slanted her head toward Aidan. "This… Tree guy…he would have tried to kill me whether I stopped or not?"

"I was afraid so." Aidan let out a tired sigh. "I did the best I could to get you safely out of the way. I hoped you'd come here and tell Eli what had happened. And you did, thankfully."

"Yes, I managed to make it here alive," Mallory said, her wry smile barely hiding her concern. "You were brave, Aidan, to put yourself on the line like that for us. And clever at that."

"I couldn't let Tree kill either of you," Aidan said. "I stopped him for now. But he's three times bigger than me, and he's mad, so he'll be back. He'll bring a lot of them with him to finish the job, too." He glanced toward the window, fear darkening his eyes. "These people do not like to lose."

FOUR

"Then we have to be ready," Eli said. "We've got officers searching for the vehicle, and we've put out a BOLO based on your description. But if he's the type who takes out hits on innocent people, he'll ditch that SUV and find another means of transportation."

He grabbed his laptop. "Aidan, I need your phone so I can trace calls to Lena. And don't tell me you didn't keep some of the text messages between you two."

"I need my phone," Aidan said, giving him what looked like a grimace of pain.

"They're probably tracking your phone," Eli pointed out.

Aidan tore into his jacket pocket. "Here."

Eli took the phone. "I'll get to this in a minute. Let's see how many navy blue SUVs of that make and model are out on the road. We have a partial plate, so we might be able to track the vehicle and get some prints at least. If he didn't switch the plates." Then he gave his younger brother a glance. "Meantime, we can narrow down any known criminals who go by the name Tree. Or Frederick."

Aidan nodded, then went to stare out the partially drawn drapes. "They know how to hide. They know how to find people. They know everything about me because I blabbed too much to Lena. And yeah, they probably did keep tabs on my phone. *Stupid.* I fell for the first girl I met in college. How pathetic is that?"

"You're not pathetic," Mallory said. "You were tricked into this by people with a lot of practice."

She got up and pulled Aidan back down. "Don't stand by the windows. They could still have us in their crosshairs."

Aidan scooted back to the couch and touched his knuckles to Koko's nose. "Cool dog."

"Koko is one of our team members and he's recuperating from an injury he received on the job," Mallory explained. "He barked at your vehicle. He knew something was wrong."

"Thanks, Koko," Aidan said. "Koko, I heard you barking when you got out of the car, too."

Koko woofed a low acknowledgment on that, his ears up and his eyes shining.

Mallory told the dog to sit. "He's still having some issues, but tonight he did try to go after that horrible Tree."

Eli nodded, his fingers hitting keys. "I called him back after Everett showed up."

Everything happened so fast after Aidan had revealed himself. Eli was still trying to put it all in chronological order.

"Did you actually participate in any of the snatch-and-grabs?" Mallory asked, bringing Eli's head up. He'd like to know the answer to that question, too.

"Nope." Aidan held both hands up. "They sure were grooming me to do that by telling me they moved certain goods through the country, to help those who didn't have much. Like Robin Hood, I guess. I liked that idea. I've seen a lot of people in need, both back in Oregon and here, too. But once they started in about what I could expect and what they expected of me, I wanted out." He shook his head. "But it was too late. They like our land, Eli. It's off the beaten path, it's a large acreage and it backs up to a big wilderness area where anyone can go missing. They know you have the deed to this place now. I can't let them take it. Or harm anyone, especially you or, now, Mallory."

"Do they know about Mom and Dad?" Eli asked.

Aidan's frown darkened. "No. I never mentioned where I came from, but they did threaten to *find* my parents." He slumped back down. "I've messed up, haven't I?"

Eli held up a finger. "You stopped in time and you stopped that man from killing anyone. That's all you need to remember."

Mallory sat with him, her dark eyes centered on his brother. "We all mess up, Aidan. These people took advantage of you and tried to manipulate you, and you realized this was wrong, criminally wrong. Now you can do something about it. You were brave to try to stop this." She smiled encouragingly. "You have us with you. We're both trained to handle this. Trained in different ways than the officers on the front lines, of course. But still, we know how this works. We've got people searching for this man, and if I know Eli, he's got someone out there patrolling right now."

Eli nodded, wondering if she'd been taken advantage of and manipulated by her ex-husband. "Everett called Helena. She's making the rounds in the woods with her K-9 partner, Luna. Luna's a Norwegian elkhound—she bites first and asks questions later. Oh, and not sure if you heard, but Everett and Helena are engaged to be married. She's an excellent trooper, but Colonel Lorenza Gallo will probably send someone to help Helena. Probably another K-9 officer."

"And we have Koko," Mallory said, smiling as the dog's ears stood straight. "He's been going through some stuff, too. But like you, he's brave."

Aidan let out a sigh. "Okay, what do we do now?"

Mallory sent Eli a quick glance. "I want you to tell us everything you can about this snatch-and-grab gang. Starting with Lena."

An hour later, Eli had a clear picture of Aidan's report, so he filed it and called Lorenza to give her another update.

Aidan had fallen asleep on the couch, Koko lying on the floor next to him. Aidan had held his hand out to let Koko sniff his knuckles again, so the dog would remember his scent and cast him as a friendly. Koko accepted Aidan now that they'd all calmed down. Now the boy and dog had a bond that would help with this whole situation.

Mallory came to sit by Eli after he ended the call. "Eli, I should go. Koko got in some good practice and he did scare the bad guy even if he couldn't corner the man."

"You can't leave," he said with such force her eyebrows lifted. "I mean, it's not safe. They probably have your license plate number, and they could know where you live already. You might go home to find your apartment destroyed or, worse, one of them waiting for you."

Mallory's eyes widened. "I hadn't considered that. Well, what do you suggest I do?"

"Stay here," he told her. "I have a small spare bedroom and Aidan likes to sleep in the loft. He'll feel better if you're here—for him to talk to if he needs someone who can act as his therapist."

Mallory stiffened, her gaze moving to where Aidan slept. "I'm the team psychologist, yes, but *you* can talk to him. You're his big brother. He seems to consider you somewhat of a hero."

"I'm no hero, but I'd like to keep you both safe," Eli replied, thinking she looked gorgeous, even in the midst of criminals and chaos. But her reaction to staying here was anything but calm. He tried again. "For tonight at least. It's dangerous out there, and the roads are a mess. Oh, and you need to know, Aidan is my half-brother." He filled her in on the details, knowing she'd understand.

"Oh, okay. I can see why you might need someone else for him to talk to."

"Yes, and you're here, so...just stay."

Shut up, Eli, his inner voice said. He wanted to argue with that voice because he wanted to keep Aidan and Mallory safe. A good excuse and a true one, but Mallory liked her privacy and she'd voiced many times she wasn't looking for a relationship.

Aidan lifted his head and chimed in, wide-awake now. "I don't think you should be alone, Mallory. They'll find you."

She moved to the fire and rubbed her hands together, but Eli knew her shivering was not just brought about by the frigid night.

"Okay, then, I guess I can stay. I'm glad I always carry a toothbrush with me. And lipstick, of course."

"Of course," Aidan said, grinning. "Your lipstick is the jam."

"Yep." Eli tried to play it cool, thinking Mallory's bright red lipstick was her trademark. They all teased her about it. "And sleep with your clothes on and have your coat and boots nearby. We might need to get out of here in a hurry." He glanced toward the front. "I have my Jeep out back, out of sight."

"Do you think it'll come to that?" Mallory asked, her voice calm while her eyes glistened with questions.

"I hope not, but you know how it is with criminals. They don't like to leave any trace of their nasty deeds."

She nodded, her arms folded against her stomach.

Could he protect both of them? He'd had training—but could he put that training to good use? He'd do what needed to be done, that much he knew for sure.

Eli sighed. He'd worry about that when it happened, he decided. He'd done okay tonight. At least, he'd gone out there and found Aidan in time to save all of them. Now he focused on trying to find a big needle in a haystack—without all the fancy electronics in his lab back at the K-9 compound. But he did have a state-of-the-art laptop and he aimed to put it to good use. Plus, he had other people within his network who could help—some legal and some questionable, but still assets. He wouldn't be picky about getting them involved.

"What are you doing?" Mallory asked him, while Aidan stroked Koko's stomach.

"I'm trying to narrow down how many Fredericks and Trees might live in a hundred-mile radius of Anchorage," he said. "We don't know the address of the main man, the boss, so that's out. And Aidan failed to really notice the address of Lena's home since she drove him there at night and he somehow didn't notice any road signs." He tapped away. "I did, however, manage to find a cell tower near a neighbor north of town. Executive-type homes, and not far from the high school. I traced a lot of calls between Aidan and someone in one particular house in that area."

Aidan sat up. "I only had eyes for Lena, but I might remember some landmarks."

"Love can be a big distraction," Mallory said on such a pragmatic note Eli knew she was off-limits in that department. Like him, she didn't appreciate anything that interrupted her work.

"Yeah, ain't that the truth," he replied. "Let's see what we can find." His fingers flew over the keyboard. "No distractions."

"That's right," Mallory said, giving him a soft smile with those lush red lips and those big brown eyes.

No distractions. None whatsoever.

FIVE

Mallory couldn't sleep.

The comfortable bed and cozy room aside, she was accustomed to sleeping in her tiny, minimalist apartment in downtown Anchorage, in pajamas, not the heavy sweatshirt and matching knit jogger pants she'd worn tonight. She loved the great outdoors, but she didn't venture deep into the wilderness. Not anymore, at least. She'd gotten lost once when she was eight years old, separated from her father while they were on a day hike. He'd been so intent on spotting a certain owl, he'd forgotten she'd trailed behind him, and she'd stayed so far behind she lost him around a curve of rocks.

Spending a night alone and afraid out in the cold, tucked into a dark open crevice, wasn't something she wanted to repeat. She stayed on the beaten paths now, even if that meant dealing with tourists wearing brand-new hiking boots that would cause their toenails to fall off.

The funny thing—no one knew this. She didn't like to talk about that scary night, so she continued to be the outdoorsy girl her father taught her to be. She could survive out there, but she didn't want to put it to the test.

That was how she felt about love, too. She might survive a relationship, but she wasn't ready to put that to the test, either. She enjoyed her work too much to waste time on love.

She thought of Eli, who'd offered her shelter. Her friend, her coworker and now her self-assigned protector. She wanted to keep him safe, too. He was a good man, and tonight she'd been reminded he was also a good-looking man. *Please, Lord, help us through this. Keep us safe.*

This felt odd. Strange, knowing Eli and Aidan were here with her. She usually liked her solitary existence. Koko snorted in his sleep, making her smile. She'd always loved animals—the main reason she'd applied to become part of the K-9 team. But she'd left out the part about not wanting to hike through dark wilderness preserves or trek over rocks and mountains to hunt a criminal. No, she'd rather explore minds and motivations than glaciers or meadows. Koko had helped her way more than she'd probably helped him. The holidays were hard sometimes. Her parents, stoic and undemonstrative, did not approve of her working in the Alaska K-9 Unit.

You could be at a large research hospital, or

running a lucrative private practice, her mother always reminded her. *We can't even discuss your work—because of the dangerous people you help put behind bars. Do you really want to live your life like that? How will you ever find a husband?*

She didn't need another husband. She also didn't want to be in some high-rise trying to help corporate raiders figure out how to make their employees work smarter. She didn't need to prove herself in that way. But she'd never thought she'd be caught in a powerful front-line attack, either, simply because she'd been coming to visit a friend. Would she be in danger from here on out?

Mallory tried every which way to analyze the situation and get a handle on what needed to happen next.

So here she lay, in a tiny room, underneath a comforter covered with bears and eagles, thinking about the man who'd thrown himself over her like a knight in shining armor to protect her. No one had ever done that before.

But then, she'd never been shot at before. Lost, yes. Shot at, no. A new perspective on surviving.

Mallory lifted the plump comforter and decided she needed some hot tea. Slipping on her boots, she carefully opened the bedroom door and headed up the long hallway to the kitchen. Then she spotted Eli and stopped. He sat alone with his laptop at the kitchen table, his eyes dancing in tempo with his fingers while the glow of the screen etched light across his handsome profile.

"Eli?"

"Huh?"

He lifted his head, lost in that deep world contained in a gazillion lightning-speed gigabytes.

"Oh, Mallory," he said, shutting the laptop so fast his coffee cup jumped. "I didn't see you there."

"That's obvious," she said, shuffling to the teapot she'd spotted before going to bed. "I can't sleep."

"Me, either," he said, ruffling his hair with his fingers. Which made it stick up all over in inky sprouts. "I've found some things."

She filled the pot and turned on the gas burner. "Such as?"

Eli pointed to the tea container by the refrigerator, then studied his notes. "I had to go deep."

Mallory spotted some herbal tea and a snowman-embossed mug. The kettle started to whistle, but she grabbed it before it got loud. Aidan had crashed up in the loft.

She settled on a chair next to Eli, her gray sweats warm and cozy, her old wool socks shifting against her legs. "Deep? Like the dark web deep?"

"Yes. I know some people."

"I'm sure you do."

He sighed and took a sip of his coffee. Setting

the cup back down, he looked her in the eye. "This is big and bad, Mallory. I'm sorry you had to get involved."

"I can handle that. Just tell me what you found."

"Apparently, this gang has hit in areas all over the state and even some in Oregon and Washington State, too. But they've never been caught, in spite of tips and conspiracy theories, even sightings. Nothing ever pans out. I can't find an official site, but articles report they have a name—Northworld SǴán or NWS."

"SǴán," she said on a gasp. "That means red snapper in the Alaskan Haida language. There's several variances, but they all have close to the same meaning." She shook her head. "As in snapping things up? Or is it a symbol?"

"Some of them like to brag. Their symbol is red with the letters NWS. Talk about being bold."

"Most criminals like to brag, sooner or later," she said. "They want to be famous, no matter how they get there."

"NWS is also referred to as *Now We Snatch*."

"How clever," she deadpanned before she took a sip of her spicy tea. "So, what do we do with this information?"

"I'm sending it piece by piece to headquarters through a secure router. They might have a tracker on anything I type, but my firewalls and security measures are pretty solid."

She sipped more of her tea. "Any word on Tree's location?"

"Nothing has come through yet. They must move around a lot, which would explain why they'd want this land—to use, abuse and then sell through a shell company once things get too hot here. Not to mention hiding bodies in the park."

Shivering at that statement, she said, "You've been busy, Eli." Now she was even more impressed with his devotion to his job. But she was concerned about his state of mind. His brother could have been killed. They *all* could still be killed.

She knew a little about their background— parents who separated and got back together, always fighting, always causing chaos. They'd had a tough life and Eli had wound up here, near his godmother.

"I don't know if I went down the right rabbit hole, but I did stumble into some social media sites—these people are legends to a lot of teenagers. I'm trying to find where they'll strike next. They seem to have a pattern of at least once a year, on different holidays."

"So they might be finished for the year." Mallory let out a sigh. "Or they're waiting for Christmas."

"That's what I think. But why risk wanting to buy this land when they've covered their tracks and stayed one step ahead of the law until now?"

"They messed with the wrong young man," Mallory replied, her gaze lifting to Eli's. They stared at each other for a few heartbeats. "Is this weird to you?"

"Me chasing down a dangerous robbery gang on the dark web? Nothing I don't do every day, right?"

"That…and me being here?"

He grinned big. "You're not weird. You're eccentric."

"Wow, is that your normal pickup line?"

His eyes flared like a match lighting. "Are you trying to get picked up?"

Another silent stare-down. "No, I mean, I was teasing. I think I was trying to tease, but I'm not funny."

He held her gaze while an unfamiliar warmth spread through her heart. Had to be the herbal tea.

"You don't have to be funny, Mallory."

But when he shook his head and went back to work, Mallory knew the tea wasn't what had made her flush. That had happened because of the way Eli looked at her.

Why had she never noticed before how adorable he really was? As in good-looking and wonderfully disheveled adorable.

"But you did a pretty good job," he finally said. "And I mean you're eccentric in a good way. I'm sorry you're stuck here, but two heads are always better than one, right?"

"Right." She wanted to say more, ask him questions she'd never dreamed of asking, get to know him better.

But the revving of an engine out on the road brought Aidan running down the stairs fully clothed, his sleep-rimmed eyes wide, Koko right behind him. That and the noise outside ended any questions she had for Eli.

"They're back," Aidan announced.

SIX

They were definitely back. Eli grabbed jackets and called out to her and Aidan. "Remember our plan. Go grab your bags! Get on your warm gear and take anything else you need. We're going to hide in plain sight."

Aidan took off like a gazelle, grabbing things as he went.

"What does that mean exactly?" Mallory asked as she rushed to get her puffer, phone and the small backpack that held her hat and gloves.

"It means we're going into the foothills behind the house. Plenty of unknown trails, but I know all of them."

Mallory stopped so quickly Eli caught her in his arms. Taking a deep breath, she asked, "In the snow and dark?"

When she heard stomping feet and crashing sounds, she knew they had to run. "Eli?"

"Yes, out there. I know those hills and this wilderness, Mallory. Aidan knows them, too. I can hide us, and I can keep us warm for a little while."

"What about the Jeep?"

Eli glanced out the back window. "Too risky to try to make it. We'll hide in the hills and sneak back to get one of our vehicles."

Mallory would *not* have a panic attack. She wouldn't show fear or weakness. Snow, darkness, shadows. Could she do this? Another loud crash and then a familiar smell.

"Gasoline," Aidan said. Koko growled low, his shackles up. "Eli, they've got gasoline!"

"Let's go," Eli commanded, throwing his backpack over his shoulders, his phone to his ear, "before they trap us in here."

The front door shook. Eli shoved them toward the loft. "I know a secret way out. Hurry." Then he spoke quickly into the phone, explaining the situation. "I need backup and the fire department, now."

He grabbed Mallory's hand, then called, "Koko, come."

The dog didn't hesitate. Koko growled low and followed Eli. Koko took the ladder after a few tries, thankfully. Eli held his phone between his cheek and shoulder while he pulled the ladder up into the loft.

"There, that'll give us some time," he told Aidan. "The secret door is inside the storage closet."

Downstairs, a window shattered. Mallory heard the hiss of fire and smelled the smoke curling up like prickly gray vines toward them. Eli's home would burn in a matter of minutes. She thought of his cute Christmas tree with the golden angel at the top.

"Eli," she said, wanting to run back and get that little angel.

"Mallory." His eyes held hers. "Go."

She crawled through the boxes and plastic storage tubs behind the secret door and followed Aidan to a crawl-through opening that backed up to the foothills.

"Follow this rocky path," Eli said. "It's hidden behind some shrubs."

"There?" she asked, breathless, as the two men secured the door with a hook and chain. The shrubs were covered with snow. She couldn't see a path.

Eli tugged her forward. "Yes, there."

The hills shimmered in a ghostly white haze. The fire blazed and the sky over the roof turned an eerie ruby-orange that contrasted brightly against the midnight clouds. She tried to shake the disorientation and flare of panic.

Eli glanced back, the fire's red-hot flames reflected in his dark eyes. "We don't have any other choice."

Then he took her hand again. "I've got you."

Mallory bobbed her head. Koko nudged her

leg, giving her a solid dog stare. She had to do this, or she'd die trying.

"Let's go," she whispered as timber crashed and embers floated all around them. She hoped the snow would dampen the fire.

Eli nodded. "We follow the path hidden by the trees and rocks. That will lead us to one of the Bird Valley Trails. We'll come out in a deep thicket and the snow will be up to our knees. These trails are usually only open through November. It's going to be cold, but, Mallory, I'll find a place to get us warm again, I promise. You won't freeze, and you won't die."

"I believe you," she said, gripping his hand. "Eli, don't let go, okay?"

He squeezed her cold fingers, but she felt the heat through the gloves she'd hastily shoved on earlier. The warmth of his touch gave her the strength to go into the white-gray abyss of snow and shadows coming at her from all angles.

"Eli, what's your location?"

Eli watched his home burning and glanced around. He named the coordinates. "About a half mile east of the cabin, in the lower Chugach Park. We're headed for Bird Creek, a trail I've hiked near my house—what's left of my house."

He watched Koko for any signs of an alert. So far, all was quiet. The woods shimmered in shades of silver and charcoal, but the heavy alder thicket surrounded the path. Looking up, he saw the tall alpines forming a canopy that protected the trails from heavy snow. "Lorenza, can they save the cabin? Is the big house okay?"

"We don't know yet about the cabin. The fire department is there. I've got two K-9 teams and two state troopers searching the area. The perpetrators got away on snowmobiles, we think."

"I haven't seen anyone out here, but we're well into the park now," Eli said, his breath lifting out like smoke in the cold. "I'm going to find us shelter. We need to get warm and drink water. Then we'll find one of the lesser paths and head northwest toward the jut-off before we reach the falls. Once we get to Penguin Creek, if I can get a signal, I'll call for someone to pick us up at the northwest overlook."

"Stay alert, Eli," the colonel said, her voice firm. "We're kind of in a fix here, with you out there. Usually, you're the one barking off stats and coordinates from headquarters, but you don't have your big screen out there with you."

"I understand. But I have Mallory and Koko, and Aidan is safe for now. I also know these woods, and I know you've got our backs because you're all familiar with the park."

"Always."

The call ended and Eli turned to where Aidan, Mallory and Koko huddled against the massive stump of a fallen tree.

They didn't have much time before hypothermia set in.

"Okay. Did you both drink your water?"

"Yes," Aidan said, glancing at Mallory. "And we gave Koko some water, too."

Mallory's teeth chattered. "Where are we going, Eli?"

"I know a campground not far from here," he said. "It's not open this time of year. Too cold and too much snow. Check your boots. If your socks are wet, that's a problem."

"I'm good," Aidan said. "The trail's not too bad yet."

Mallory nodded. "I wore my tall boots and layered my socks." She checked the K-9. "And I had traction footpads for Koko in my tote."

"Smart," Eli said, never doubting she could handle this even if her dark eyes had flashed panic when they had exited the cabin. He'd marched them through heavy snow and cold woods to get to this hidden trail. Only the locals knew about it, and Eli was familiar with every inch of this part of the park. "There's a campground about a fourth of a mile up the way," he said. "We'll find what we need there."

"Like a latte and a warm bed," Mallory quipped as she finished her water.

Eli took the water canister back. "Sorry, not that nice, but shelter and warmth. How does that sound?"

"It's a spa," she said, standing. "Let's go, and while we're walking, explain to me how you plan to get us out of this. Or rather, how *we* can get us out of this."

Eli admired her fortitude. "We need warmth and a snack," he said. "Then we hydrate again before we take off toward the west and turn to head the backway down to a rest area, where I hope we'll be picked up by friendlies."

"Good plan," Aidan interjected. "Let's do it."

"Yes, let's do it," Mallory said with a half-hearted lifting of her fist. "And, Eli, thank you for saving our lives back there."

He shot her a wry smile. "You're welcome. Let's see if I can keep it that way."

SEVEN

Mallory sat huddled inside a cavern Eli called *shelter*. She wasn't so sure about that, but at least the U-shaped little cave did provide sanctuary from the heavy snow coming down in twinkling white flakes. He had a fire going just outside the open door. She knew the fire brought warmth, and it would also keep the winter predators away. She didn't want a run-in with a lynx or a moose tonight. They needed the warmth, but the downside was that the fire could also bring human predators.

She touched a hand to Koko's warm coat. The K-9 had been amazing. She wondered if she'd gained his trust enough. Dogs might not have the same emotions as humans, but if they suffered the same trauma, then psychologically, that showed emotion, at least to her way of thinking. Being here in this scary, fast-moving situation had turned out to be the best possible training for the dog's return to work. He'd stayed near Mallory, obeying her while Eli's faint pocket flash-light and the brightness of fresh snow guided the path ahead of them.

The campground Eli had tried to find had proved too difficult to maneuver. They'd been forced to stay on the trail, or risk getting lost. Eli handed her a collapsible tin mug with hot tea in it, bringing her mind back from the shadows threatening to overtake her. "Here, it's herbal but at least it's warm. Eat your granola bar."

"Thanks," she said, taking a bite of the chewy peanut-butter-and-chocolate snack. "How do you manage to have all these supplies in your back-pack?"

"I keep it packed and loaded with whatever I need if I decide to come out here," he explained. "Like a go bag. If I get in the mood to take off on a hike, I'm ready, and now, I have my lap-top in there, too. Not that it will help us much out here." He stoked the fire with a big, jagged limb, then looked at the path down below. "So far, we're okay."

Mallory felt safe with him and Koko. Aidan seemed to go with the flow, but right now he had a lot to deal with. She'd prayed that she and Eli could help his little brother out of this mess, while she sat there trying to thaw her hands and feet.

She expected Eli could figure things out even without modern technology. "So you like to camp out?"

He stopped to give her a surprised glance. "Who doesn't?"

She stared up at him, wanting to tell him the truth. But she didn't want to add the worry of her fears to his already growing list of responsibilities. She had to carry her own weight and help him, not hinder him. "Right. Always fun. I've been working so much lately, and with it being winter now, I haven't done much hiking."

"We'll have to remedy that," he replied. "Once we get out of this situation alive, of course."

"Of course." She should be thankful instead of whiny. "You're an amazing man, to get us away from a burning house and bring us on a safe path to get help. Koko is holding his own, so I guess our experiment shows he's on the mend."

Eli lifted his chin toward Koko. The dog sat silently beside Aidan and Mallory. "A trouper. Who knew our night would go so wrong?"

"I did," Aidan said, his head down, his arms wrapped around his knees where he sat against the cavern wall. "I almost got you killed, and now, because of me, your cabin is toast."

Eli didn't say much on that subject, but Mallory saw a flash of pain pass through his eyes. "We're alive," he told Aidan. "And we're going to get back to civilization and start fresh tomorrow on trying to nab these dangerous people."

"I'm in on that," Aidan said.

"No, you won't be in on that," Mallory replied

sternly. "We'll need to hide you and put someone on you for protection until this is all over."

Aidan scowled at that. "I can stay with one of you. You're protection-type people."

"No," Eli said. "You need to be far away from us. Too dangerous."

The young man started to say something, but Mallory held up her hand. "You're on their hit list, Aidan. For the unforeseeable future, you have to stay hidden. It's our job to make that happen and your job is to do as we tell you—so don't be stupid."

Aidan's eyes widened in an obvious new respect for Mallory. "Okay, I get it. All right."

"Good," Eli said. "Let's eat, get watered up and get moving. Like you said, Aidan, they'll find us if we hang out here all night."

After Eli killed the fire with snow and stomping, they gathered up their gear and headed out, but Mallory had a bad feeling. The sun wouldn't come up until around 9:00 a.m. That meant they had at least six more hours of nighttime to get through. The temperature was hovering at twenty degrees Fahrenheit, and the wind chill even lower.

If the bad people didn't do them in, the weather surely would. Pushing away the shadows huddling in the growing darkness, she instead began to estimate how much longer they might survive out here. They had to stay moving and warm.

If they lost body temperature—seventy degrees or lower range—they'd die. That could happen within just a few minutes.

She tried not to dwell on that. They were covered from head to toe and the warm cave had helped. Now she marched along the snow-covered, winding trail, and uttered silent prayers for all of them.

She'd never wanted to be in this situation again, but she planned to survive this night just as she'd survived that other night so long ago. She owed Eli that much, at least.

They made it another half mile when Koko lifted his head, stared into the woods near the creek and alerted. Eli stopped, holding up a hand.

"Do you hear that?" Aidan asked, the sound of a revving motor echoing out over the blanketed trees.

"Yeah." Eli held a finger to his lip. "Someone's on a snowmobile. Between us and the path I need to take to get us out of here." He listened close. "But they can't go any farther on that thing. It's too dense where we're going."

Another roar sounded out on the path. Eli pivoted around. "They're trying to surround us, cut us off. We'll need to make a detour."

Mallory held tightly to Koko's lease. "I don't think they're friendly."

"No. They tracked us by following the creek

somehow, but that water is icy cold and mostly frozen. People rarely come this far in during December."

"Unless they're looking to kill someone," Aidan whispered. "Got any suggestions?"

Eli didn't answer. He seemed to be calculating in his head. "Okay, we're going deeper into the woods."

Mallory stood and tightened her grip on Koko's leash, her mittens covering a pair of gloves. She was weary, but she refused to give in to the panic that tried to slap her down and paralyze her. "Let's go, then."

When they heard voices echoing over the thicket, Eli rushed them off the path. A flashlight's high beam hit into the air, hovering on them like a spotlight.

Then a shot fired out over the tranquil countryside and singed a tree's massive trunk about a foot from where they'd stopped to take cover. Shattered pieces of bark and wet snow drifted around their heads and showered them with cold, icy fingers.

"This is bad, isn't it?" Aidan asked, a shudder in his voice.

"Yep, buddy," Eli said as he pushed them into the woods off the trail. "But we're not going to let them win." He helped Mallory position her tote bag onto her back. "Let's go."

They took off through the snow and bramble,

not caring if snow got inside their boots. More shots rang out, spraying debris all around them. Mallory glanced back, expecting to be overtaken. Then she turned forward and followed Eli into the dense darkness of the snow-covered wilderness.

EIGHT

Eli had to get his bearings. If they got lost, they'd never survive. But the snow had changed things in all directions and made it hard to hear anyone following them.

When the sound of a roaring engine growled through the trees below, he decided he'd take his chances. "Let's go west," he whispered, staying behind Mallory while Aidan trudged beside her. "We'll veer left at that huge spruce jutting out onto the path. I'm fairly sure the turn to the west should be up there."

"How sure is fairly sure?" Aidan asked, his tone just above a shiver. "I'm not familiar with this area."

"The falls will be hard to miss since they'll be mostly frozen over. We'll need to cross the creek near a deep spot, but they could be waiting on the ice to ambush us."

"Speaking of ice," Mallory said. "How do we cross it without the proper traction boots?"

"Very carefully," Eli retorted. "We'll stay close to the shore until we find the road out."

"And if we don't?" Aidan asked.

"We will, one way or another." Eli didn't plan to let anyone freeze tonight, and he sure wasn't going to let them die.

They crunched through packed and fresh snow, frozen tree limbs and twigs. Eli stumbled and righted himself. Koko remained in his working mode, his footpads giving him some protection. The dog dealt with this trial by fire—or ice in this case—in a professional manner, the way he'd been trained to act. He stopped now and then, lifting his nose in the cold air. That gave Eli a hint that someone could be following them, but he couldn't cover the deep snow tracks they had to make to get away. Too dangerous to try.

When they reached the spot he'd been searching for, he pointed up. "See the falls. Just a trickle now. They'll freeze solid before the month is out."

Mallory glanced up to where a white mass sparkling with icicles all the way down to where the waterfall ended, and the vast creek began. "Wow, if I weren't running from killers, I'd be in awe."

"Same here," Eli replied, glad she still had a dry sense of humor.

"We need a plan," Mallory said, puffs of fog dancing around her.

"I *have* a plan," Eli replied, not sure what his plan actually provided.

"I mean, a plan if we get attacked. You brought your Glock, right?"

He nodded. "Yes, I've had it with me in my shoulder holster since they arrived last night. So that's a plan, I guess."

"Aidan and I can find limbs and rocks to throw at them or hit them. We can fight and Koko can attack."

"All good to know," Eli said, thinking, except for Koko, that might be a bad idea. "Koko can hold them off."

"But we can help," Aidan said, already jumping on Mallory's suggestions. "We won't leave him, right?"

"No. Hopefully, he'll scare them away long enough to give us time to make it to the pickup spot."

"He can at least maim them," Mallory said on such a pragmatic note Eli shot her a wary glance.

Koko's head went back and forth, his nose up while he waited for someone to give him a command.

They made the turn and Eli stepped ahead and scanned the dark horizon. A clear white shimmer caught his attention. "I see the creek."

They hurried down a bluff, dodging falling snow and rocks. His whole body had become numb from cold, but he couldn't think about that now. Mallory let out a breath and he turned to check on her. "You okay?"

"Fine. Just hit a stump. I think my socks are wet. Both pairs."

"We'll need to get you out of those boots soon."

He didn't have to tell her about frostbite. Anyone who lived here knew the perils of dealing with frostbite and hypothermia.

He silently prayed that God would lead them to safety. Bettina would tell him to keep going. The motors roaming behind them told him he didn't have any choice. When the motors cut off, he knew their pursuers were now following them on foot.

He saw the vast wide part of the creek below. "We made it!" he said, turning to check on Mallory and Aidan. But then his elation turned to bone-chilling fear when he spotted a shadow lurking on the curving hillside, about fifty yards behind them.

"Let's go," he commanded, practically dragging Mallory down toward the ice-crusted water.

She held on to Koko, and the big dog growled an alert. "They're behind us, aren't they?" she asked on a winded breath.

"I think I saw someone, yes."

Aidan tumbled down the hill, fell, then got up. A gunshot lifted into the air and bullets hissed near where he'd fallen. "Think? No thinking about it. They're after us."

Eli motioned. "C'mon." The only way they could go now was by following the frozen shoreline or taking the shortcut across the widest part of the creek—the part that wouldn't be all the way frozen yet. The ice could crack, and the people after them would have a clear shot.

They had nowhere to hide.

Mallory ducked while gunfire sounded through the trees, her heart pounding fearfully with each step. Koko didn't like it, either. Afraid this would throw him back into conflict, she kept talking to him softly and patting him on the head whenever they stopped for a breath. "You'll be rewarded greatly with a nice prize, I promise," she said after she tried to take a deep breath. But the cold air hurt her lungs.

"Keep moving from tree to tree," Eli said. "If you see anything you can use as a weapon, go for it."

Searching for a big limb kept her mind off the shadows reaching toward her like cold tendrils. A good solid limb could give a person a good solid head injury, or at least a damaged face.

She found her chance when they rounded a twist in the landscape. The broken limb almost tripped her, but she called to Eli.

"Hold on." Then she handed Koko's leash to Aidan and managed to lift the small yard-long log off the snow. "It's sturdy," she said. "I can make this work."

Aidan searched around and found a smaller branch and a five-inch jagged rock and dropped it in the deep pocket of his parka. Then he cleaned off the foot-long log. "I'll try this one. Throw it in their face."

"Not if they have a gun trained on you," Eli replied. "But it could come in handy. I have two flares. I'm saving them to alert the team that we need help. But I could use one to blind someone." He handed one to Aidan. "Take care of this."

"Anything that works, man," Aidan said, tugging at his fur-trimmed hood. "I'm freezing."

They stayed just off the shoreline along the creek. "We'll only go over the creek as a last resort," Eli told them. "It's deepest here, and not as stable, so we'll have to be careful."

The ground was too slippery. If they got stuck, they would be a perfect target for a sniper. Mallory's teeth chattered, but she held her head up to study their surroundings.

Eli tried his cell again. "Still no signal. The old back road isn't far from here. The colonel planned to get someone in here to watch for us, based on my coordinates. We just need to find their location."

Aidan shook his head. "With this weather? Who would try?"

"Our team," Eli said. "They won't leave us out here."

Eli wiped ice away from his skin and squinted into the curve. "I see the road ahead. It curves away from the creek."

Aidan did a fist pump. "Yes."

Mallory let out a sigh of relief.

Koko woofed.

Eli turned to them. "We need to cross that little stretch of ice to get there."

Aidan and Mallory looked at the deep part of the creek and then back to him.

"It looks a lot bigger than it is," he said. "It's only about fifty or sixty feet wide, but it's the best way to get there from here."

He guided Mallory ahead and then looked at Aidan. "Hold one hand on her shoulder and follow her toward the shore across the way, okay?"

Aidan did as he asked, bobbing his head. "I won't let go."

Mallory rolled her eyes. "I'm perfectly capable of getting across the ice by myself if I have to. I can handle following the shoreline once I'm close."

"That's the idea," Eli replied. "Just stick together, okay?"

"What about you?" Aidan asked.

"I'll cover you." Eli checked the surroundings. Then he reached inside his parka and pulled out his pistol. "Get ready, and whatever happens, you both keep running. Hear me?"

Mallory shook her head. Eli couldn't defend himself alone. "I'm leaving Koko with you."

"No. Just go, Mallory, and take Koko with you."

Up above them, snow showered down and rocks crashed onto the frozen water. "Go!" he repeated. "We don't have time to argue."

NINE

Mallory and Aidan ran, with Koko growling and barking beside them, trying to warn them. Gunfire blasted the night, causing the K-9 to snarl.

"We know," she said, giving him the quiet signal. Koko went quiet but kept his nose up and his ears perked. Mallory tried to stay calm. "Aidan, how are you?"

The young man huffed a foggy breath. "Just great. I can't believe I got my brother in this mess."

"We'll find a way out of it," she said, turning to search behind them. "Where did Eli go?"

Aidan stopped, panic-stricken. "We can't leave him back there alone. They'll kill him."

Mallory nodded. "You're right. Hold on to your limb and that rock."

They turned back on the trail. When they heard footsteps up ahead, Aidan tugged Mallory behind a jutting, craggy rock face. Koko growled low.

"If it's not Eli, we attack," Mallory whispered.

Aidan bobbed his head, the darkness etching his face in charcoal and gray.

Footsteps moved in a stealthy cadence through the snow. Mallory waited, her heart beating like a loudspeaker churning out their location. Where was Eli? Why had this happened? She'd tried to do as he'd asked and keep going, but she couldn't leave him. She'd fight to the finish to help him.

Starting with making sure to stop whoever was stalking them. She looked at Aidan. "Get ready."

Aidan nodded. He had the sharp-edged rock in his hand, and she had a limb with a knobby knee at the end, much like something a Viking would wield.

She prayed for strength.

The shadowy figure covered in a parka approached, glancing here and there, his body crouched, a gun in his right hand. She shook her head. "Not Eli."

Aidan gripped the rock.

Koko shook with anticipation, his body trembling. "Attack!" she commanded after she unhooked his leash.

Koko hurled his body against the gunman, grabbing his leg with a tooth-first hold. The assailant, dressed in heavily insulated pants, screamed in pain and fell to the ground. Aidan held the rock up and aimed it at the man, hitting hard against his shoulder, causing him to drop his weapon. The man shrieked, expletives echoing out over the night.

Aidan grabbed the gun while Mallory lifted the branch of wood and slammed it against the assailant's head.

"Tell me who sent you," Mallory said.

The man twisted and groaned.

"I'll get the dog off, after you tell me."

"Wolf," he said on a weak whisper. "Wolf."

Then he passed out.

"Release," Mallory commanded, winded and full of adrenaline. "Guard." Koko stepped off the man and stood sentinel. That rock had made their pursuer hallucinate. No wolves around here.

"Did we kill him?" Aidan asked as he eyed the man in the same way he might stare at a big bug.

"We knocked him out. He'll have a severe headache when he wakes." She gingerly checked his pulse. "But he will certainly freeze to death in a matter of minutes. Weak, but alive." Then she searched him for weapons and identification. "If help arrives, they might be able to save him and question him."

"He won't talk." Aidan glanced up the hill. "What about Eli?"

Koko's ears shot up and he snarled. Then they heard hushed, cushioned footsteps moving up the way. Koko sniffed high and let out a woof.

"I think that might be him," Mallory said, pocketing the man's wallet and an extra magazine full of ten-round 9mm bullets she'd found in his hidden inside his coat.

Aidan held up the gun. "Should I take this weapon?"

"Absolutely," Mallory replied, thinking she was becoming too tough and jaded. Glancing at the shock on Aidan's face, she said, "Give me the gun."

He stared at the heavy weapon and then handed it to her. Then he exhaled a long breath. "That was intense."

Koko did a low whimper. Mallory shoved Aidan back behind the rocks. "Let's be sure it's your brother."

They crouched there, freezing, tired, weary. Mallory held the gun ready and prayed for Eli's safety, for *their* safety, and she also prayed for the man who'd been tracking them. She hated to harm another human, probably why she wound up in the psychology department of the K-9 unit. But…she'd do what was needed to keep them all alive.

Then she peeked around the rock. "Eli. It's Eli!" She stood and waved, relief warming her. "We're here."

Eli rushed toward them, glanced at the unconscious man lying in the snow, then said, "Let's go. We'll need to take the ice."

"Why?" Aidan asked, running behind his brother.

Eli pointed back toward the hillside and bluff. "Because of them," he replied, as three men came barreling around the curve.

"Move as fast as you can over the ice. If you slip, get up or crawl if you must." Eli glanced back. "Remember the penguin shuffle." He held his gloved hands out and up and turned his feet outward. They needed to run but running on this tricky ice would be almost impossible. They all had on rubber-soled snow boots, but no add-on stretch traction devices.

"Skates," Aidan said as they slid onto the frozen lake. "We need...skates." That last word stretched as he hit the ice, skidded, then tumbled.

Eli managed to turn and lifted Mallory so she could find her center of gravity. Aidan's legs curled and crumbled but he got up and kept pushing.

Koko didn't want to move, but Mallory tugged him gently. "C'mon, boy, your pads have traction," she coaxed. "Koko, come."

The dog took a couple of hesitant steps, lifting his covered paws high, one step and then another.

"Good boy," Eli said. "Koko, you are a hero in my book."

Aidan glanced back toward where they could hear men shouting. "I've done this all my life," he said. "Why can't I get moving on the ice now?"

"You're too nervous," Eli told him, aware of

the people tracking them from the shore. "Slow down, take a breath. Focus on finding your balance. Shuffle and take small steps."

"I need to take small runs," Aidan said while he wobbled like a top.

Eli's phone dinged. Slowly and while he kept moving and balancing, he lifted it out of his lower parka pocket. "Cavalry is here," he said, stopping to raise it to his ear.

"Eli, where are you?" Lorenza's voice had never sounded so good.

"We're on the lake, treading ice," he replied, relief washing over him.

A round of shots dinged and hissed, hitting the ice around him, blasting and spewing cold chips into his face like slivers of glass. When he heard a crack, Eli shouted to Mallory and Aidan, his phone to his ear, "Run. Just run. We're almost to shore. Help is waiting. Use the flare."

"We're on our way," Colonel Gallo said. He could hear her sending out orders.

Mallory commanded Koko to go and shouted the same command to Aidan. "Get to the shore," she told him. "We'll be safe now."

Eli stood still, gauging his situation. He crunched down, balancing his feet so he could take off quickly. After he watched Mallory and Aidan manage to scrape and crawl up to the shrubs hugging the shore, he braced to make a run for it before the ice caved and took him with it. The sound of voices coming from behind him warred with the shouts he heard in front of him. Another shot hit close to his left leg. It was now or never.

The sound of the cracking ice splitting all around him forced his hand. Then the last thing he heard was Mallory calling out to him, "Eli, hurry!"

TEN

When Mallory heard other dogs barking, she knew the team had found them. "Aidan, go and show them the way." She took off toward the water, shouting as she ran, Koko with her.

"Eli," she called, bullets whizzing as the three men moved deftly across the ice, getting closer and closer. *"Eli?"*

She saw him bob up in the middle of the ice, his hand flailing through the air, his heavy clothes dragging him down. Glancing behind her, Mallory heard voices but didn't see anyone coming. He wouldn't last long in that water, especially with his heavy clothes and boots working as anchors. How deep was the water there? She had maybe five to ten minutes to save him, but how?

She looked around and saw a huge piece of driftwood. If she could drag it out to the water and send it sliding toward him, he might be able to catch on to it. Mallory tugged at the cold, snow-covered log, her gloves slippery now. Koko danced around, giving her an idea. She told him to stay and took his leash. She attached part of it to the tree and looped the rope around her arm. Then she tugged, adrenaline giving her strength. What had taken only minutes seemed like hours as she pulled the log up and then pushed it toward the water.

She could hear the men getting closer even as they slipped and huffed over the ice. At least the cracks had made them rethink chasing Eli. They shot several times, but due to the shadows and distance, thankfully missed Eli and her.

"Koko, play," she said, hoping he'd want to tussle with the leash rope. She yanked at the rope. "C'mon. *Play*."

Koko barked and got the idea. He let out a yelp then bit into his leash. Mallory dragged the log while his tugs helped pull it along. His strength and the idea he was having playtime made the job go faster.

"Thank you, Koko," she said, winded, her skin burning with tears and cold. "Halt." Koko let go, his eyes shining brightly. This dog had amazed her all night. One brand-new giant play toy would be in Koko's future.

Once they had the crusted, cold log pushed into the water, she called to Eli as he clung to a chunk of ice. "Eli, try to hold on to this so we can get you out."

She was about to go into the shallow water

to shove the old wood toward him in the deeper middle, when a strong hand clamped her on the shoulder. "Mallory, let us take over."

She turned to find Gabriel Runyon bending down to help her up. His Saint Bernard, Bear, waited nearby. "Go get warm. We'll get Eli, I promise."

Noting Gabriel was dressed for this kind of stuff, Mallory could only nod, exhaustion taking over. But Eli was still out there. "He's there," she said. "Those guys are almost to him and he's been in there awhile. Don't let him die."

"We won't," another voice called out. Brayden Ford, a former navy diver, and his K-9, Ella, a Newfoundland trained in water rescue, came running up. They were followed by EMTs. "We're going after him."

A moment later, Everett Brand raced to her side and guided Mallory to a hilltop parking lot by an old road.

"We found the road," she kept mumbling. "We did it."

"You sure did," Everett said, his arm around her to keep her from collapsing.

One of the paramedics threw a heavy blanket over her. Then they got her inside the ambulance and tugged her out of her soggy boots and socks.

"Where's Koko?" she asked Lorenza when she stepped into the ambulance. "Where's Aidan?"

"Koko is being checked out in another bus,"

the no-nonsense colonel told her. "And Aidan is fine. He's covered in a blanket, drinking strong coffee and lots of water. He did a good job of getting that flare up."

"Thank you," Mallory said as an accommodating EMT checked her vitals and asked her about any injuries. "I'm not hurt, but I'm so tired."

"We'll get all of you to the hospital to check for frostbite and injuries. I'm surprised hypothermia didn't set in," Lorenza said, glancing toward the attendant.

"We were prepared," Mallory said. "Eli made sure we had food, water and fire. Then they found us."

"It's okay. You'll be okay," the colonel said.

"Go see about Eli," Mallory replied. She couldn't sleep until she knew he was safe. "And Lorenza, catch those awful people."

The colonel touched a hand to her arm. "You know we will."

Mallory lay back, but the sound of more gunshots blasting through the woods didn't give her much comfort.

Eli felt light and free. He wanted to let go and just sleep, let the icy water take him. He was too tired to muster the strength to grab onto the big log a foot or so away. But he heard dogs barking. *Dogs. K-9s!*

He lifted his head, his gloves wet, his hands

bruised and bleeding from the jagged ice. Someone called his name. He watched as the log moved toward him. Then Ella's bark pierced the air. That meant Brayden was nearby. "Hey, girl. Good girl. You found me."

"Eli, grab on, buddy." Brayden appeared out of nowhere, his dive suit on. "I got all dressed up for this?"

"Sorry," Eli said. "No dive necessary." He started to slip but Brayden broke through the ice, carrying a rescue buoy with him.

"Hey, don't take a nap. We've got work to do."

Someone else crawled, inch by inch, toward him, all bundled up. Gabriel Runyon, covered in a parka and heavy wading boots.

"Hey, grab the buoy," Brayden said again, staying nearby. "We'll tug you out."

Eli tried to reach the buoy, but saw the log clearly now, and he saw Gabriel stretching across the ice with a rope.

Brayden came up beside him. "Eli, I'm gonna tie you to the buoy and give you a shove toward the log, okay? Hold on to whichever one you can."

Eli's eyes fluttered. Sleep. He only wanted sleep. His hand slipped off the orange buoy.

"Grab the log." Gabriel told him. "Hurry now."

Brayden nudged him. "C'mon, Eli."

All of a sudden, a surge of adrenaline went through him. He wasn't going to die, after all. With one last ounce of breath and renewed energy, he tugged at the log, the promise of warmth coursing through his system. After several tries and with Brayden guiding him, he finally connected to the rustic piece of driftwood, a lifeline. Then he felt something else. Reaching for the dark ribbon, he realized it was a dog leash. *Koko!* He remembered Koko and Mallory, trying to help him. Where were they now?

Once he'd pulled up enough to hold tight, Gabriel called out. "Okay, man. We're going to pull on the log, so hold tight."

Eli nodded and forced his upper body across the splintery driftwood. "I'm...r-ready." Why did he sound so weak?

Brayden sloshed through the water like a salmon on a river run. "Okay. Hold tight."

Then more sounds. Gunshots. Bullets hitting the ice and dinging all around them from every direction. Return fire coming from the shore. Eli held on, thinking of Mallory and Koko, and Aidan. He grunted as the guys tugged at the log and got a good hold. Then, once it was on solid ice again, Eli bounced but held on, the log moving at top speed.

He took in a breath of air, his lungs burning with cold, his body so numb he wasn't sure if he'd actually made it out of the icy, frigid water. But soon, he felt hands lifting him, felt the comfort of a blanket being thrown over his body. He looked up, watching the sky, so broad and bright, as the tip of the crescent moon moved with a slow soft grace through the velvet clouds.

"Am I gonna live?" he asked anyone who might hear.

"Of course, you're gonna live," Brayden said. "Was there ever any doubt?"

"Yeah, a lot," he retorted. "Mallory?"

"Being looked after," Brayden said as a paramedic took his vitals and started whisking him away.

"Koko? Aidan?"

"All good," Gabriel told him. "We have to finish up here and then we'll see you at the hospital?"

"Hey, what about the bad guys?"

"Working on that, too, Eli," the colonel said as she moved by, her short hair shimmering white and gray in the dawn. "You concentrate on you. That's an order."

"Yes, ma'am." Bossy, his boss.

Then he was surrounded by machines that beeped and EMTs who barked orders louder than a K-9 could bark at a criminal. They tugged at him in all directions, getting him out of his weighted clothes and boots.

Eli smiled and thanked God. "I'm impressed someone found that piece of driftwood," he mumbled.

One of the responders nodded. "Yeah. We heard

your friend Mallory and her K-9 dragged that thing out onto the ice."

"That figures," Eli said as he began to drift off. "They make a good team."

ELEVEN

Mallory heard the gunfire, but the EMTs kept her inside the ambulance, and soon they had her en route to the hospital in Anchorage. Koko was on his way to Dr. Cora Madison's office. The veterinarian worked full-time with the team's K-9s. She'd check Koko over, and hopefully Mallory would have him back soon.

That is, *if* they allowed that after what had happened tonight. She'd had to get special permission and go through training updates to temporarily handle Koko, but it had been one of the joys of her life. That and having a chance to relax with Eli outside of work. Well, they didn't actually relax last night.

"Eli?" she asked, her mind fuzzy as drowsiness took over.

"He's safe," the attendant told her. "His ambulance should be right behind us."

"The gunshots?"

"Can't answer that, but the K-9 unit, the park rangers and the state troopers are all in on this."

"That's good." Mallory allowed the wonderful warmth to seep through her. She'd survived another night in the cold, dark winter. But this time, she hadn't been alone out there.

When she woke up, she was in a hospital room with an armed guard at her door. Panic clawed at her, making her want to tear the tube out of her arm and run.

She glanced around the warm, sterile room and spotted a person sitting in the recliner beside her bed. "Eli?"

When he didn't respond, she decided she must be dreaming. Other than being cold and wet last night, she was okay. So why was she in the hospital?

"Eli?" she said, louder.

His eyes flew open, and he jumped straight up. "Yeah, I'm here. Are you okay?"

She had to smile. He had bandages on his face, scratch marks on his jawline and gauze wrapped on his hands. And he was worried about *her*?

"I think I'm good," she said, her voice croaky and raw. "What did they say about you? Shouldn't you be in your own hospital bed?"

He sat back down and crushed his wild mane with his wrapped hand. Then he lifted his foot. He wore bright blue hospital socks, bandages peeking here and there. "I have some frostbite on my feet, but it should be all right. My hands are shredded from clawing at ice. A tad of frostbite on a couple fingers, but I still have all my fingers and toes, at least. My throat hurts and I'll probably wind up with a head cold, but they've checked me over and I hope I'll be released today."

"Today?" She looked out the slit in the blinds. "How long have I been here?"

"At least twenty-four hours," he said. "The colonel made us stay overnight. Aidan is fine, so she took him to her house." He shrugged. "Poor kid is shaken. They shot and killed one pursuer last night, Mallory. But the other two managed to get away. That's why we have that guard at the door."

She glanced at the burly officer while she let that settle in. They were still in danger. "What about the one Aidan and I knocked out?"

"We think he's the one they took out. He was kind of slow and wobbly on his feet, from what I've heard."

"Identification?" she asked. "I had his wallet in my coat." She pointed to the locker across from the bed.

Eli got up and searched her parka. "It's in there. We'll get someone in to bag it." He held up his bandaged hands. "Don't want to mess with it myself."

Mallory nodded. "We can get it to the lab, and

they might be able to lift some prints." Then she asked, "What do we do now, Eli?"

"I don't have a home right now," he said somberly. "It needs extensive repairs, and we can't stay there for obvious reasons."

"We?" She hadn't planned to stay anywhere near that place.

"They want you and me in a safe house, under guards at night. During the day, we go to work—the best place to stay safe and help with the investigation."

"And Aidan?"

"Uh… Lorenza seems to have taken him under her wing. He goes where she goes, for now. Next thing we know, she'll have him wearing power suits, too."

"Aidan isn't a suit kind of guy," Mallory said, smiling again. How did Eli manage to make her smile in the midst of all this danger and chaos? "I think it's sweet that she's helping him. Denali and he should hit it off."

Eli nodded. "Yes. That husky could use a good buddy." Then he gave her a direct glance. "Aidan and I weren't close until recently. I'm glad he trusted me, you know?"

Mallory's heart went out to Eli. "I'm glad, too. When you're better, when this is over, we can talk more, I hope."

He nodded. "I knew you'd understand."

"What about Koko?" Mallory asked, sitting up.

She wouldn't push him on his relationship with Aidan right now.

"Koko is with Doc Cora, being spoiled rotten. She soaked his paws in warm water, put some Musher's salve on them and deemed Koko a hero. But the whole team has promised to put him through his paces once he's clear, so he doesn't go all brooding on us again."

Mallory blinked, refusing to cry. "I love that dog."

Eli leaned up in the chair, his eyes holding hers. "Mallory, he's okay. Doc says this little adventure could have propelled him on the right path. He didn't have time to think about his anxieties."

"Good. Neither did I," she replied. Her eyes burned, maybe from the cold she'd endured, or maybe because she felt like a failure, and needed a good cry. "I never dreamed this could happen. They might not let me mentor a dog again."

Eli stood again and rushed to her bed, then touched his bandaged hand to her face. "Hey, this is *not* your fault. I've been thinking about a lot of things since they brought us here. This was meant to happen, Mallory. This is an evil organization that preys on young, impressionable teens and young adults, and we almost lost Aidan to them. Lorenza is looking for Aidan's now-ex-girlfriend Lena Matson. She seems to have disappeared off the globe."

"A lot of places to hide in Alaska." Mallory sniffed. "Where are we hiding? Where's the safe house?"

"I don't know yet," he said. "Right now, you need to rest." His blue eyes, so like a deep stream, moved over her face. Analyzing and assessing— that was what they both did for a living.

Mallory couldn't consider the way he looked at her as anything other than Eli making sure she was all right. "What about you?" she asked. "You were in the water a long time, Eli."

"Not too long, thanks to you and Koko. Mallory, you risked your life to save me. I'll never forget that."

Gratitude—just another way of him being nice. Nothing more.

"I couldn't leave you. I sent Aidan ahead with the flare."

"So I heard. My little brother apparently goes deeper than I realized. You're both on my admiration list."

Admiration. That was okay. She could live with that. She wanted Eli to admire her, didn't she?

Mallory lowered her head. "I had to think fast."

"Well, you did a good job. Brayden said another five minutes and I wouldn't be here. Sending that old log out saved them those precious minutes of trying to get to me, and that's why I'm sitting in your room now."

"Did you come to visit and find me asleep?" She had to ask.

Tugging at a big robe, he said, "Uh… I couldn't sleep, so I came to check on you and… I didn't want to leave."

She wouldn't try to figure this out. Not yet. "You fell asleep in the chair?"

He gave her a sheepish smile. "I guess I did."

Before they could finish staring each other down, the door came open and Aidan and the colonel marched into the room.

"Well, you two look cozy," Lorenza said, her razor-sharp gaze leaving nothing to doubt. "Feeling better, are we?"

"Yes, ma'am," Eli replied, backing away from the bed.

"I just woke up," Mallory admitted. "I need coffee desperately."

Eli couldn't get out of the room fast enough. "I'll go find some."

"Eli, shouldn't you be in bed?" the colonel asked sternly.

"I'm better." He kept going at a surprisingly fast pace, considering he was wearing those funny-looking socks, and limping. "Oh, Mallory has the dead guy's wallet in her parka. Can you bag it?"

"I'll get right on that," Lorenza said, grabbing some tissues from a box on the table by the bed.

Aidan's amused expression bounced from Mallory to the colonel. "Did we miss something?"

Lorenza shook her head. "No, but we came in on something. Not for you and me to worry about right now." She held the black wallet in the tissue. "I need to get this to the lab ASAP."

Mallory let out a sigh. "Eli was just checking on me. We're both happy to be alive."

"Me, too," Aidan said. "And I have the best protection in town." He thumped toward the colonel.

Lorenza rolled her eyes. "Speaking of protection, I assume Eli's told you our plan."

Mallory nodded and adjusted her hospital gown. "Yes. I'm good with working all day, but a bit concerned about going to a safe house each night."

"It's a remote place, but easy to surveil," Aidan blurted, causing Lorenza to lift an eyebrow.

"Thank you," the colonel said on a dry note. "And don't go around repeating that."

"I know the protocol," Aidan said, nodding, his fingers doing an invisible zipper over his mouth. Then he shrugged. "That's all I know. She won't read me in on the location."

Another lifted eyebrow and just a hint of a smile. "Aidan, my new shadow, is correct. You'll have guards around the clock and escorts to get you to and from work."

Mallory wasn't about to protest against guards.

But around the clock with Eli? Could she handle that? She didn't have much of a choice, though, did she? She'd have to do some serious praying and hope God would help her break this down into a workable acceptance.

When Eli returned with coffee and a muffin, she appreciated him even more. He seemed to know exactly which foods she liked.

She dove into the blueberry muffin and enjoyed the crunch of sugar crystals sprinkled on top, while Eli and the colonel talked strategy. That gave her time to admire Eli's dedication to his job all over again.

But it also gave Aidan a chance to wink at her and smile big, meaning he'd seen her doing all of that admiring.

The colonel's phone buzzed, bringing Mallory out of her thoughts.

"I see. Okay, let's find out."

Lorenza ended the call. "We think we've located Lena Matson, possibly in Fairbanks. I need to get back to the office." She indicated to Aidan that it was time to go but turned back to them. "I'll send an escort to get you both checked out and in a safe place."

Aidan nodded and followed the colonel toward the door, obviously in awe of the woman. "Is Lena okay?" he asked, his tone more subdued now.

"I don't know," Lorenza replied, a hand on his

arm. "I know you cared for her, but, Aidan, she's dangerous. You understand?"

"Yes, ma'am."

Eli glanced at Mallory. "He's holding it together, but he might be in for a lot of hurt once the excitement dies down. Finding Lena's a start. We're going to keep at this, Mallory. And… Lorenza is willing to let Koko stay with us at the safe house."

Mallory bobbed her head while she almost choked on a blueberry. At least, she'd have Koko as a buffer between her and Eli—and these strange currents of awareness heating up her whole system. Like Aidan's hyper excitement that could crash and burn, she knew her growing feelings for Eli could bubble over and make a mess of things. She had to avoid that at all cost, for two reasons. One, she liked him as a friend and didn't want to lose their friendship. And two, she didn't want to take that leap of faith and fall too fast into another man's arms.

TWELVE

Eli checked his surroundings, making sure they had a guard at the front and back doors. This small cabin located in a remote village of about three hundred people was one of several safe houses the K-9 unit used to hide people in danger. Eli had heard of the place, but he'd never had to actually stay here. Off the grid, but not completely. They had running water pumped up from a nearby stream and indoor plumbing, which wasn't always the case with some of the local cabins.

When he came back into the small den, he found Mallory working to light the pile of kindling she'd crammed into the potbellied stove.

"Let me help," he said, the shadow of one of their guards hovering out on the enclosed front porch. The other one had his Jeep pulled around back, hidden by trees but with a clear view of the house.

"I've got it," she said, the hiss of a flame backing her words. The fire flared to life. This small place would be warm soon enough.

Noticing how she held her arms in a protective stance across her midsection, he had to ask, "Mallory, are you okay with this?"

Her chin jutted out in that cute way. She was summing up the situation. Summing him up, too. Eli had realized something while sleeping in that chair by her hospital bed. This woman meant more to him than he was ready to admit. A slight crush from afar was one thing but being with her in such an intense way was quite another. She was sweet but tough, strong but vulnerable. Pretty and smart and… He could go on. Her heart had been broken. Could he fix it?

Mallory stood staring at him with those big brown eyes, her dark lashes like black silk. "I'm not sure how I feel about this. No one ever tried to kill me before."

She'd missed the question's meaning, which could probably be good. No need to get into what they could be feeling. She might not sense the connection he'd felt since she'd rushed into the cabin. Way too much going on to think about anything emotional. They had a case to crack.

"Me, either," he said. "I've been with the team a few years and… I'm always stuck down in my lab. I stay busy all day searching for ways to help find criminals."

She smiled. "And I'm usually up in my office,

trying to figure out humans who go bad, or help-ing humans who do good."

"We rock at our jobs, don't we?"

Her laughter was nervous, unsure. "Right now, I'm not feeling that."

A knock at the door caused both of them to whirl. The guard opened the front door. "Colonel Gallo to see you."

Mallory let out a sigh of relief. "I'm too jittery."

Eli couldn't blame her. Despite the guards, he kept looking over his shoulder.

Before his boss made it inside, Koko came running toward them, his tail wagging, his ears perked up. He had a doggy smile on his face as he ran from Mallory to Eli.

"Someone's missed you two," Lorenza said on a dour note, even though her eyes held a slight twinkle.

Mallory bent down to stroke the K-9. "Hello, Koko. You feeling okay?"

"He's fine," the colonel said, her shrewd gaze scanning the cabin. "He'll be your third guard."

"Thanks, Lorenza," Eli said. "How's Aidan?"

"Surrounded by a couple of our officers and watching hockey." Her smile disappeared. "I have an update, but I don't want Aidan to know this yet."

Glancing at each other, they both gave her their full attention. "We're listening," Eli said.

"We located Lena Matson, the girl who got Aidan involved in this ring."

"That's good," Mallory said. "I'd like to interview her."

"I'm afraid that won't be possible," Lorenza said grimly. "When the team got there, they found her dead."

Mallory gasped. "*Dead?* That's awful. Aidan will be devastated."

"That's why we haven't told him." The colonel moved to the fire. "Eli, I want you to do as much research on that girl and her family as you can. Here and at work tomorrow. They obviously killed her because in their minds, she failed."

Mallory nodded. "She meant nothing to them. She was only part of the chain of command—on the bottom ladder."

"Exactly," Lorenza agreed. "If they'd kill her over this, then they will certainly keep coming after all of you, especially Aidan. I'll have to find the right time to tell him."

Mallory paced the small den. "What about her family? Aidan said her father is involved in this."

"We don't know yet," Lorenza said. "We can't locate him. Aidan remembered some landmarks, but not the actual neighborhood. We have her phone records, and once you're back in the lab, we can get a warrant for her father's records, based on probable cause due to Aidan's statement and their text and phone messages. We haven't found Tree yet, either. Maybe you two will have better luck tomorrow."

"We'll get on this tonight," Eli said. "I didn't have much time or equipment at the hospital."

Not to mention his laptop being soaked in freezing water. Thankfully, someone had brought him his work laptop. He'd saved his research from the other night to that one, too.

Lorenza studied the room, her gaze checking every corner. "What you sent got us started. I've got several people on this."

"Any help from the ID I found on the guy who died last night?" Mallory asked.

"Yes," Lorenza replied. "He was wanted in three states. I'm sure he came to Alaska to hide. His name was John Rockmore. He also went by the name Johnny Rock." She moved away from the fire, her steps timed like a soldier's. "Unfortunately, we have nothing solid to connect him to the NWS."

"I'll find something," Eli replied, his mind whirling.

Mallory gave him a sharp glance. "We'll work on finding something, anything, to help us."

Colonel Gallo eyed both of them. "And you two are okay here, together?"

Eli looked at the floor. "Yes, sure."

Mallory's chin jutted out another notch. "Of course."

"Safer together," Lorenza commented after assessing both of them. "Keep in touch."

She left the same way she came in, quickly and efficiently.

"What did she mean by that?" Eli asked, hoping this would be an opening to the obvious tension in the room.

Mallory's hair fell across her face like a curtain. "I have no idea. We're perfectly safe here—with each other, right?"

Eli shrugged. "Yep. And we have work to do."

Mallory stroked Koko's golden-brown head. "Let's get on it."

But when she looked up at Eli, her eyes full of questions, she didn't seem so sure.

Mallory closed her laptop and rubbed her tired eyes. She'd read up on snatch-and-grab robberies across the country, studied cases that had gone to trial, and tried to find a way to put together some sort of profile on these people.

Did they do it for the money, or for the challenge, the thrill? All three, she decided. They liked the money but fencing expensive jewelry and other merchandise would prove risky. They had a system, but she couldn't find one yet.

She wished she'd been able to talk to Lena Matson, but the girl had paid for her part in the NWS. Did her father even know she'd been killed?

"What are you thinking?" Eli asked, shattering the comfortable silence from moments earlier. While his hands were still bandaged in places, he'd put smaller Band-Aids on his fingers so he could peck with one or two fingers.

"I'm wondering about Lena. How could a father put a child through that—make her a criminal, force her to work for him and his nefarious boss?"

"You know how the world works," Eli replied gruffly. "Not all parents are wonderful."

"What about you?" she asked, then wished she hadn't.

He took off his glasses. "What *about* me?"

"Your parents. You talk about Bettina a lot, but your rarely mention them."

"That's because they rarely raised me," he said, his head down. "My father was an alcoholic and my mother enabled him. They got divorced and then I found out I had a half-brother, conceived when my father and mother were apart. They got back together and raised Aidan or pretended to raise him. His real mother abandoned him when he was little. He doesn't know her. We didn't always get along, but we love each other. End of story."

Mallory let that soak in, understanding making her sit up. "So you became an overachiever—the firstborn child always does—and you have a sense of duty to your younger sibling. And you're helping to put him through college."

Eli turned from the table and poured himself more coffee. Then he walked over to where she sat on the plaid couch, Koko at her feet.

He took a chair next to her. "I am that, but I also had to be the adult in our house. Aidan's had some issues, but he's in college now and he *was* doing better. I'm worried how all of this will affect him. I took care of him most of the time, growing up."

"Ah, that explains why you and Aidan are becoming close now. You still want to take care of him."

Slanting his head, he said, "Are you trying to analyze me, Dr. Haru?"

"I'm trying to *understand* you," she replied. "In a personal way, Eli. I'm not tight with my parents, either. They're stoic and serious, so my home was always quiet. Too quiet. They love each other and they love me, but I had more fun at my friends' houses, where chaos reigned."

He grinned at that, and her breath caught in her throat. The man was handsome and a bit mysterious, like a spy who'd been hiding in plain sight.

"You like chaos, huh?" He waved his arm in the air. "Chaos brought us here." His eyes held hers. "Together."

Mallory couldn't read him, but something flickered in that dark blue gaze, some message she couldn't quite decipher.

"This is a different chaos," she said, confusion coloring her words. "I'm still grasping…everything else."

"Meaning me?"

She was about to answer when Koko stood up and growled low.

Eli reached for his weapon, then stood and headed for the door. The moment was lost. More concerns, more chaos. But no real answers from him. Not yet. And no time to get away from whoever was pursuing them.

THIRTEEN

Eli waited inside by the front door so he could make sure the guard was safe. But when he glanced through the blinds, the man wasn't there.

Mallory came up behind him, Koko next to her. "What do you see?"

"Our front guard is missing." He scooted around her and looked out back. "The Jeep's still there, but I can't be sure the other guard's in the vehicle."

Mallory pulled out her phone. "I'll call."

Eli waited near the window, listening.

"No answer from either," Mallory said, her phone to her ear. "This can't be good."

Then they heard shouts and gunshots. Koko growled, his ears going back while he stood ready to go.

"I'm going to check," Eli said. "Koko, come."

"I should go with you."

"Let me see what Koko and I can find," he told her. "Stay here."

Mallory stood staring, her pulse pounding a jittery beat. What if she didn't *want* to stay here?

She searched the cabin and found a fire poker—cliché, but sturdy. It could do damage. Then she spotted a cast-iron skillet near the stove. The thing was heavy, but she could also use it as a weapon. Placing the fire poker by the door, she waited with the skillet.

Silence held her in a death grip. They'd just survived freezing temperatures and criminals chasing them. What *now*? She'd pray. She hadn't prayed in a while, but maybe God understood silent prayers better than a rant.

She heard more gunshots. The back door rattled.

Eli? When she heard Koko's bark echoing over the frozen woods, she headed to the door. Eli would still be with Koko unless he'd been shot.

Trying not to panic, she stood in a corner by the door with the frying pan gripped tightly, her breath held until she went into deep breathing.

The door slowly opened enough for her to see a meaty hand and a dark parka. Not one of her men. Not Eli.

She waited a heartbeat and let him move past where she hid, then she turned and aimed the heavy skillet at the man's head. With a primal grunt, she hit him hard on the back of his wool cap. He fell to the floor, groaning, his hands grasping for her.

Mallory threw the frying pan against his head, causing him to scream. Then she grabbed the poker and slammed the sharp prongs into his hand as it inched toward her boots. "I don't think so."

The man writhed in pain, one hand wrapped around her boot. "Stop it, lady. I'll kill you."

"I'm not going to be ladylike with you," she retorted as she slapped the poker at his hand and tried to twist away. "And you're not going to kill me."

The man managed to roll and grab her with both hands, tripping her. Mallory screamed as he rose and hovered over her, his face now dripping with blood, his gaze like a wild beast.

"You're dead," he shouted, dragging her down, his big body a dark shadow, his hands reaching for her neck.

If she could make it to the open door....

Mallory clawed at the man's face, but just as his hands circled her throat, a pile of brown-and-black fur leaped through the air. Koko went for the man's already hurting arm, his snarl aggressive and sure.

Mallory stood, her breath coming in gasps. Finding the poker, she grabbed it and held it against the man's chest.

The big man kicked and screamed. Eli rushed through the back door, both guards behind him.

He let out a long breath, his hands on his knees as he bent over. "I was afraid he'd hurt you."

Mallory waited until the two officers surrounded the man. "Koko, release, halt."

Koko immediately let go of the man's bleeding arm and stood watching, his teeth bared in a dare.

"I'm okay." She had a death grip on the poker. "I'm okay."

Eli gently took the poker from her. "That I can see," he replied, noting the blood on the weapon. "One down, but two got away."

"We'll have to move again?"

"Maybe not. I don't think they'd try to come back here."

"Me, either," she said, wiping her hands together as if to clean them. "We do make a good team."

Eli looked at her, really looked at her, his eyes holding hers, his expression creased with wonder and awe. "Yes, we do."

An hour later, they sat by the fire with Koko, letting him enjoy his playtime. The guards had called for someone to come and take in the man they'd captured. He'd kept screaming about his rights and excessive force, but he could settle that with Colonel Gallo.

Hopefully, someone back at headquarters would get him to talk. Eli wanted that to happen, and fast. Being secluded with Mallory was almost as difficult as being chased by dangerous people. A lot nicer, though.

"We have his DNA, thanks to your sword-play with that skillet and poker," he told Mallory. "Even if he won't talk, between that and his prints, his future isn't looking so bright. He'd be wise to cop a plea."

"Another great save," Mallory said, giving Koko a high five with her hand on his lifted paw. He endured that, and then went back to his doughnut-shaped squeaky toy.

Eli let out another sigh while he watched how her eyes lit up when she was with Koko. She'd turned all warrior woman and taken down a man three times her size. Make that two men, if they counted the now-dead one she and Aidan had halted in the woods. "How is it that they can find us, but we can't find them?"

Mallory shook her head. "You were working on something before they came in, right?"

"Right. Lena's father, Mitchell Matson. He's a lawyer, pillar of the community, churchgoing. What am I missing?"

"Those are all fronts," Mallory replied. "He has all the markings of a sociopath. Too good to be true."

"Ah, that makes sense. His poor daughter properly hung on his every word."

"What about the mother?"

"She's a teacher—upstanding, volunteers,

lots of friends-and-family type pictures on social media."

"I always look at people's friends to find out about them," Mallory admitted. "You can learn a lot sleuthing on social media. It's like one big tell-all gossip session."

"We are of like mind," he replied. Mallory was perceptive, intelligent and resourceful. She'd masterfully used the fire poker and skillet against the intruder while Eli's heart had almost burst with fear that she'd be attacked and killed. But she was a strong woman.

She sent him a questioning gaze. "Eli?"

He sank back against the couch. They were safe again, and the guards had done their jobs. The shift switch had gone as planned. He could relax and enjoy being with Mallory.

"I was afraid something had happened to you. But you handled it like a pro."

She blinked and her expression changed from wondering to acceptance. "Oh, *that*. I was fine." Then she shook her head. "Actually, that's not true. I was terrified you and Koko had been hurt. When I heard him barking, I was so afraid you'd been shot."

"As you can see, we are both right here, safe and sound."

"I'm thankful for that," she said. "I said lots of prayers on your behalf."

"That's good to hear," he said, thinking they

were of like mind in that department, too. "Bettina turned me into a believer, but she didn't preach to me or demand I clean up my act. She simply lived her faith and her actions rubbed off on me."

Mallory smiled at that. "My grandmother taught me about the Bible and God. My parents are agnostic, at best."

Eli nodded and rubbed Koko's fur.

"You can handle yourself," he said, careful with his words. Then he yawned. "Wow, I'm more tired than I thought…and really worried about Aidan. We barely had time to talk. I'm glad Lorenza took over with him. She's good at bringing out the best in people." Shrugging, he added, "I don't know what I'd say to him right now, anyway."

"I understand," Mallory replied. "You're having a letdown from the adrenaline. Now…the shakes will come, along with the fear of being so close to death. It's natural."

"Yes, but it's also natural to care about people," he said. "The team, our K-9 unit, is like family to me. Family, that's what all of you mean to me."

"Of course." She looked down, her hand stilling on Koko's furry coat, her eyelashes fluttering when she looked back up at Eli. "I feel the same way. I love my work. I've become friends with so many. I've never appreciated that more than I do right now. Friends help us through the worst of times."

Eli looked at her as realization hit him. "Yes." Without thinking, he grabbed her and kissed her. A quick peck, but a real kiss. "You're brilliant, Mallory."

She drew back, her eyes darkening with surprise. "Thank you, I think."

"I'm sorry." He'd just kissed Mallory. Had he overstepped? "But you're onto something." Aidan hung around with a lot of students at college. If we can find one of them and ask the right questions, that might lead us to find answers.

Mallory relaxed, but touched her hand to her lips. "Oh, of course. That's a good idea, Eli."

"You gave it to me. You mentioned the importance of friends. Your brain is always on task."

"That's me," she said with a brittle laugh. "This brain—can't slow it down."

Eli didn't regret kissing her—but it had only been a little peck. It didn't mean anything, right? Then why did he feel disappointed in the way she'd responded. Was she mad that he'd kissed her? Or did she like the way it felt, too? He'd find out because he planned to kiss her again.

And soon.

FOURTEEN

The next morning, Mallory and Eli finally made it back to headquarters, Koko accompanying them. They'd had no more visitors last night, but Mallory hadn't slept well. Someone wanted them both dead, and Eli had kissed her.

It was reflex action. She knew that. But his lips touching hers in such a quick, sweet, intimate way had set off all kinds of signals. It had also generated a warning.

She'd been married to a man who'd charmed her into believing she counted in his life. How could she trust anyone in that way again?

And yet, Eli was so easy to trust. He wanted to take care of her, but he acknowledged her ability to do that for herself.

His gestures, his actions were so different from what she'd endured with Ned Kent. But Mallory guarded her heart the way Koko guarded a criminal.

Now, she sat in her office going through profiles and old cases similar to this one, waiting to hear on news about Lena Matson's mother, Rhonda. No one could find her. Mallory was also awaiting word from a college student who'd shown up a lot on Aidan's social media sites. Maybe he could give them some clues.

Eli knocked on her door. She hadn't spoken to him much this morning. Cranky without her coffee, she smiled when he handed her a tall cappuccino.

"Can you read minds?"

Koko rolled over and waited, as if expecting a treat. But he got fed regularly and only had treats once or twice a day. When he didn't see anything interesting, he grabbed his plastic squeaky bone and laid his nose against it, his eyes on Eli.

Eli laughed. "I can read a woman who needs more than a fast cup of black coffee on the way out the door."

"We did leave in a hurry," she said. "I'm glad we talked Lorenza into letting us bunk here for a while."

"Makes sense," he said after he took a swallow from his own cup. "We can get a lot of work done after hours."

She hadn't considered that. She'd thought being here, back in a professional environment, would give them some distance. But working here alone at night, not so much.

The second shift could be her buffer. Koko

helped, too. The dog had been protective of her since the night at the cabin. They'd bonded in so many ways. Koko had been trained in crossover protection. He'd certainly earned getting back on the team.

Putting her random thoughts in their proper boxes, Mallory took a long sip of her coffee. Eli handed her a bag containing a huge cookie.

"What? You were holding out!"

Koko's head came up. He obviously felt the same way.

"It's oatmeal raisin, from your favorite place up the street."

"Did you sneak out?"

"No, I had it delivered."

"Do you have any more surprises?" she asked after taking a bite of the cookie. Eli somehow always knew what she liked.

"I have information from the colonel. Will that count?"

"Yes." Back to business. "What is it?"

"The DNA from Poker-face Man," he said, pulling out his phone. "You took down Tree, Mallory. With a skillet."

She dropped her cookie. *"What?"*

"Yes. Frederick Turner, aka Tree. You nabbed him."

Mallory sat stunned. Then she smiled. "Can we tie him to the boss?"

"I'm thinking yes," Eli said, giving her that

dark-spy look that made her turn all soft and mushy. "His rap sheet reads petty stuff and grand theft and felonies, of course. He and the man from the woods—John Rockmore, aka Johnny Rock, were tight and…they are on Mitchell Matson's payroll. Bodyguards."

"Not very smart ones," she retorted. "One dead and one in jail."

"The dead one can't talk, but Tree was singing like a talent show contestant."

She shook her head. "That bad, huh?"

"Worse. He's not happy about taking the fall. Matson headed straight to the Cayman Islands— without him."

"Really? Offshore accounts?"

"Probably, and fencing whatever he's managed to sneak out of the country. But Tree says most of the *goods* head straight in the other direction— the Bering Sea. You know—Japan, China and Russia." He bit into his cookie. "There's more, but he's lawyered up, and suddenly, he's not wanting to talk much anymore."

"Unbelievable," Mallory said, her heart hurting for Aidan. "What if they'd taken him, Eli? They could have easily put your little brother on a freighter and we'd have never seen him again."

"I know," he said, his jawline tight. Mallory could see a distinct pulse beating there. "Lorenza's watching the kid like a hawk. She knows if they get to him, he'll disappear forever." He gripped his coffee cup. "I intend to stop them for good."

Remembering Lena Matson's death, Mallory asked, "So, what happens now?"

"Lorenza's put out the word on Matson. His daughter is dead, his wife is missing and he's gone AWOL. Tree says the wife was devastated that their daughter had been killed. Supposedly, she left him."

"Or so Tree says."

"Yes." He finished his coffee. "Lena was shot. Ballistics matched the bullet to the same type bullets they found around the lake. Tree swears it wasn't him. That is, before he shut down."

"I should talk to him," she said.

"He's fighting for a plea bargain now. So yeah, he knows more." Eli shrugged. "But he thinks someone higher up got to Lena. Tree is claiming that Matson double-crossed the boss. They didn't like him bringing his daughter into things. He's given us a lot, but Tree knows more than he's telling."

"Well, yes, but we want him to open up and give us specifics." Mallory stood. "Let's get permission to question him."

"No." Lorenza's stance remained firm. She held a hand on Denali, her K-9 partner, who stayed by her side and had become the team's mascot. "Mallory, you can question him about his feelings, get a read on what motivates him and hope his issues make him squeal the truth. I'll go with that. But, Eli, you don't need to be in the middle of that. You can observe and take any information to help with your searches. But Aidan is your brother which makes you way too close to the situation."

"Okay," Eli replied, knowing when to let go. Mallory mumbled in agreement. "Can we also talk to Scrawny Kid, the one we found on Aidan's social media—David Joiner. If we locate him?"

Lorenza's gaze told him she didn't like that idea, either.

"No."

"I'll assign someone closer to Fairbanks on that. I need you two here, doing what you do best. Got it?"

"Yes, ma'am." Eli replied. Lorenza was right, of course.

"You need to find out more about this teenager. Aidan was a bit cryptic on how they know each other, but it's not through college. David Joiner dropped out. So do one of your searches and see if you can locate him before going down a snowy rabbit hole."

"Got it," Eli replied. "If he's been coming and going for a while, he might have run into Lena Matson here or there. He might have mentioned Aidan to her—to get them together."

"And she could have singled Aidan out," Mallory added. "Aidan is the perfect profile they look for. New to school, lonely, shy, confused. Needing to prove something to someone, hoping to find a close-knit group to fit in with. And a bit awkward."

"That's Aidan." Lorenza sat staring at her desk pad, her fingers rapping against the wood. "Okay, let's try locating this kid first—I'll talk to the Fairbank authorities and you keep digging here."

Then she held up a finger. "Wait." She stood and wiped her hands down her suit. "I think it's time I tell Aidan the truth about Lena." Glancing at Mallory, she said, "You can help in that area. He might need you."

"I'll do whatever I can," she replied softly.

Eli nodded. "Thanks, Colonel. We'll get online and dig a little more."

"Good," she said. "Meantime, work up your report and keep building our case. Matson will mess up sooner or later. He's desperate and he's grieving. He has nothing to lose at this point."

"Got it. He's dangerous. We'll find all of them, including his boss."

"That would be a good Christmas present," Lorenza replied. "And, Eli, take Koko with you whenever you leave this building. He's officially cleared to work."

Eli hurried with Mallory through the building toward the interrogation room, then watched her go inside. She looked as cool as river rocks and she was just as tough. He, on the other hand, worried that Tree would do something to harm her. Ridiculous, since he was handcuffed to the table.

Eli remembered that quick kiss he'd given her, right on the lips. A stupid move, but the feeling of kissing her hadn't left him. He'd like to try again and keep his lips on her just a little longer. Mallory didn't seem so sure about that.

Her ex had obviously done a real number on her. She'd always been reserved and quiet, but now she gave Eli the kind of distant glances that told him she wasn't sure about him.

He'd have to show her she could trust him. The woman had saved his life, after all. That meant she cared a little bit.

Eli would win her over. They'd been coworkers for a long time. Now he wanted more. Maybe he'd *always* wanted more, but he'd never acted on those feelings. But almost dying in a freezing lake could do that to a person.

He stood behind the two-way mirror and enjoyed watching her do her thing. Mallory could decipher feelings, emotions and minds, while he could decipher biometrics, Wi-Fi codes and cell phone technology.

They made a perfect pair.

But someone needed to convince Mallory of that.

FIFTEEN

Mallory came out of the interrogation room, her mind whirling with the tidbits she'd drawn out of this criminal. Tree had been tough to crack, considering she'd been the one to bash his head in, but she had found a tear in his nervous evasiveness.

"He used to live in Fairbanks," she told Eli. "That's when he got involved in this gang. Bad home life and he needed some quick cash to get away. NWS gave him a home and a purpose."

Eli scoffed. "Yes, I heard. His purpose is to snatch and grab, rob and loot. A familiar story."

Mallory's eyes blinked and refocused. "He inadvertently slipped up. He called the leader a name that stayed with me. Big Wolf."

"Big Wolf," Eli checked his notes. "Got it. Let's go to the lab and I'll do some digging."

"What time is it?" she asked, panic settling over her. She avoided the basement where the lab was set up. No windows, no light.

"Late," Eli replied. His phone dinged, as if on cue. He put it on speaker. "Lorenza?"

"Eli, Aidan says the boy is in and out of school and likes to party a lot. He's in some pictures with Aidan online, but your brother doesn't think he's connected to Lena."

"Thanks," Eli said. "How's Aidan?"

"He was shocked and a bit angry that I kept Lena's death from him, but he's a strong kid. I ordered pizza and Denali is comforting him. He also said he can contact David and feel him out, but I'm debating that since any contact could be tracked."

"Tell him we'll see him soon," Eli said. He glanced at Mallory after the call ended. "Aidan's been through so much. We can't let him down."

"We have to find a connection to David Joiner, Lena's dad and this Big Wolf."

"That's our assignment," he said. After they took Koko from a handler, they headed down the elevator to the lab. "She'd rather we surf the web instead of trek through the wilderness. Considering how well that went the first night and all."

"Good point," Mallory said, her expression filled with apprehension.

Eli shot her a worried frown. "You don't like the lab, do you?"

She held her hand tight on Koko's leash. "I don't like the dark. You don't have windows down here."

"I'll give you light," he said, turning on switches. "Is that better?"

Mallory stopped and held a hand to her throat. Those words—*I'll give you light*—got to her. No one had ever said that to her before. She knew Eli meant them literally, but her heart took them in the Biblical way. She needed light in her life. Eli gave her that. He made her laugh. He listened to her drone on about criminals and their minds. He cooked her chili and brought her favorite cookies and coffee.

He was a friend. But standing here now, watching him turn on light switches with an indulgent smile, made her see he was more than a friend. Could she trust him on that?

"We can go back upstairs," Eli said, jarring her mind back to work.

"No, no," she said, shifting on her boots. "Thank you."

He shrugged. "When my lady asks for light, I produce it."

She giggled. Really giggled. No one had ever said that to her, either. "You're a clown *and* a prince."

Koko watched her and then looked at Eli. This dog could sense the tiniest of shifts in the mood.

Eli bowed, his blue eyes shining with a brightness that left her breathless. "At your service." Then his eyes went dark. "I'm always here, Mallory. You should know that."

Mallory's giggles evaporated, to be replaced with something she couldn't define. "I do now," she whispered. "I see you, Eli."

He let that settle over him, a questioning look moving like slow water through his eyes, then said, "Let's get to work."

Leaving Mallory to wonder if he saw her in the same way. Or if she'd just embarrassed herself by saying silly proclamations to him.

How would things feel after the adrenaline rush of being chased by horrible, deadly criminals faded away? She suspected they'd go back to normal. Passing in the halls, comparing notes, having quick lunches together with others, arguing over epic movies and active cases. The friends-at-work type things.

But now she wanted more.

Mallory sighed. There was too much going on. Her mind clearly wasn't working on all cylinders.

"I'm in," he said, pulling her a chair up to his many computers and contraptions. "Let's get this done."

"I'm ready," she replied, seating herself in the tall chair beside him after she'd told Koko to stay. Eli had easily slipped back into work mode. She should do the same. But she wasn't ready for all these new feelings dancing through her brain.

Eli stared at the screens blinking in front of him. "It's like a maze," he told Mallory.

She sat calmly going through all the twists and turns, taking her own notes. Koko slept at her feet.

Who would have thought brave, confident Mallory didn't like the dark? Maybe that explained why she'd sat at the very edge of the cave they'd found the other night. Another thing about her he'd catalog. That and how she'd said, *I see you, Eli.* What did that mean? That she'd never noticed him before, or that she saw him as more than a friend now? Maybe he could ask her that, later, when they weren't trying to save the world.

Mallory studied the screens. "It's the usual criminal pattern. A cultlike following, getting recruits off the streets, through word of mouth, and going after messed-up teens and disillusioned young adults. They brainwash these needy humans into doing their dirty work. Aidan was smart to get away."

"Except he knows things, thanks to Lena. They have to eliminate him."

"And us," she replied. "Let's go over the details."

"Well, these images I found after checking Aidan's online accounts do show David Joiner. He's in a picture with Aidan from a few months back. If I go to David's page, he's also friends with Lena. Several pictures of them together, but not at school." He pointed to an image on the big screen. "And look at the tattoo on his arm."

Mallory pushed up her glasses and stared at the screen. "A wolf—*Amarok*." She looked over at Eli. "That's the local word for *wolf,* or one of the many variances. That could connect us to Big Wolf." Then she gasped. "Eli, the man Aidan and I knocked out—the one who didn't make it—he kept mentioning a wolf! I thought he was hallucinating, but he tried to give me a name. Wolf. Big Wolf."

"Now we're getting somewhere," Eli said, tapping the keys. "Let's go back to NWS—Northworld *SGán.* We know *SGán* is a variance of red snapper. So we have wolf and fish."

"And Amarok could be the name for the leader," Mallory added. "Let's switch to what you found in Fairbanks."

Eli brought up another screen. "No surnames to bring us to that." He kept typing. "I'll look for any organization or business names connected to that."

Mallory waited, a yawn sneaking through her lips. They'd been at this awhile, comparing everything, but she wouldn't stop now.

"Look," Eli said, pointing to a name. "NW Contractors. Owned and operated by Red Graystone."

"Northworld Contractors? Big Wolf?" Mallory asked. "Or Red Snapper. Anything? Wolves are gray."

"Either way, this is the closest we've come to

finding the head honcho." Eli grabbed his hair and tugged at it. "He's a prominent member of Fairbanks. Philanthropist, married with a family and he owns contracting businesses all over Alaska."

"One in Anchorage," Mallory said, pointing to the screen. Then she pulled up the medical examiner's notes on Lena. "Look, Eli."

He read the notes. "Small tattooed name on left shoulder. *Amarok.*" Then he went back to the report on her father. "He worked for NW Contractors—Manager of the Anchorage branch."

Eli hit keys and turned to Mallory. "I just sent it all to the colonel. We'll need to locate David Joiner, and we still need to build our case on Red Graystone, but it's a start. We've connected some dots between Mitchell Matson, Tree, and Red Graystone, plus David Joiner and Lena Matson. But Mitchell and her mother are still missing."

"We could end this soon," Mallory said, glee in her words.

"Yes." He hugged her. "We do make a good team."

She held him close and then pulled back, her dark eyes full of mysteries. "You're amazing, Eli."

Eli gazed into her eyes and then he kissed her, this time in a soft, sweet, lingering way, to ensure she wouldn't bolt. Then he stepped back.

"And you're the best." She looked so surprised he panicked. "I'll go find some coffee and chocolate to celebrate."

When he came back, he found Mallory asleep, curled up on the small futon he used whenever he needed a nap. Koko lay on the floor, guarding her. The dog had a crush on her, too. She looked like a beautiful doll, lying there with her hair curling over her cheekbone.

He grabbed an old superhero afghan and carefully placed it over her. He stopped for a moment to take in the woman who'd been forced to hang with him for the last few days. Through shootings and a fire, then ice and snow and now back to work. They'd been through every emotion imaginable in a short time, and they'd come close to death. *But we survived.* Eli thanked God for that.

God's time, Eli. Bettina's words floated through his mind. *If you're patient and stay true, God will give you what you need, not always what you think you want or need, but what He knows you'll need.*

"I need you, Mallory," he whispered.

Mallory sighed in her sleep. Peaceful.

With the light shining down on her.

He sat and watched her sleep, thinking they'd learned a lot about each other these last few days. He wanted her in his life. All the time.

Eli read over some notes while he kept an eye on her.

Tired, he leaned his head back against the chair and drifted to sleep, his mind on Mallory. Then he came awake. Overhead, an explosion boomed, causing the building to shake. Screams echoed. Footsteps hit the street above them.

Mallory sat straight up, her eyes wide. "What's going on, Eli?" Koko stood and barked, his ears up, his nose twitching.

His phone buzzed. "Colonel?"

"Eli, get out of the lab. Aidan called me. He got in touch with David Joiner—against my orders—and learned they've set bombs at headquarters. We've taken David into custody. They're coming after you and Mallory. Go *now*! I read your report, and we've located Mrs. Matson. I'll explain the rest later."

"Understood." Ending the call, he turned to Mallory. "Let's go. Something just blew up."

"They've found us again?"

"Yep. And this time, they've endangered the team and everyone else who's working here right now."

SIXTEEN

Eli hit the elevator buttons again. "Not working. Let's take the stairs."

Mallory clung to Koko, giving him gentle commands. "Go. Halt."

Koko followed her lead, proving his merit in chaos yet again. He'd been through fire and ice. Could he handle this?

Could *she*?

Eli opened the door to the stairwell. Smoke fumes puffed out, followed by a hot wind.

"Nope. Can't go that way."

"What about a door leading to the street?" Mallory asked, glancing around.

"No doors to the street. We can't have anyone breaking into the lab."

"So the only ways out are blocked."

"Yes," he said, his gaze roving the short hallway by the stairs. "Well, there *is* one way out."

"Where?" Mallory wanted to get upstairs and

help the others, yet at the same time, she wanted to keep Eli, Koko and herself safe.

He pointed down.

"Down?" Her heart raced ahead, causing her to gulp. "Eli, what's down below this floor?"

"A tunnel," he said. "We don't use it much, but it's an escape. They found it when they renovated a few years ago. The dogs sometimes train in it."

"The dogs." She glanced at Koko. "Do you think he'll be able to go through this tunnel?"

"He's trained to do what we command him to do. And we don't have much time. Are you okay with this?"

When they heard gunshots above, Mallory didn't have a choice. She'd have to face her worst fears and follow Eli out of here.

Eli shoved away a cabinet and tugged at the hidden door, then turned to motion to Mallory. "Let's go."

She tugged on Koko's leash and gave him the command. "Go."

The dog sniffed the dank air inside the dark hole then turned to stare at her. Did he sense her fear, her hesitation, the terror taking over her mind?

"Mallory, we don't have much time."

She looked at Eli, then she looked into that dark abyss. "I...can't."

His eyes widened. "It's the only way. We don't

know what's going on up there. The whole building could be on fire."

"Eli, I want to, but I got lost from my father once on a hike and I spent the night in the dark, in a small enclave." Her hands shook. Koko started to whine. "I still have nightmares sometimes. And panic attacks." And now she had to face a real nightmare.

Eli took Koko's leash, realization in his eyes. "Mallory, I'm so sorry. You don't like the dark, as in claustrophobia?"

She bobbed her head. "Take Koko and go without me."

"I'm not leaving you," he rasped. "I understand you're scared, and I wish you'd trusted me enough to tell me. But I can't leave you. If you stay, we all stay."

She couldn't let that happen. "I should have been honest," she said. "I didn't want to be judged." She'd tried so hard to be tough and she'd done okay until, until *this* happened.

"I would never judge you," he said, his eyes on her despite the noises coming from upstairs.

"You have to go," she insisted. "Koko can help. I'll stay here and wait for someone. Or I'll figure out another way."

"There is no other way," he said. "Mallory, you need to trust *me*." He reached out his hand. "I'll find the light for you. I'll make sure of that because I've fought against my feelings for you—

but that's over now. We need to stay alive, so we can really *live*."

She wiped at her eyes and said a prayer. Then she reached out her hand to Eli.

Just as the main door to the lab burst open.

"Now!" Eli said, dragging her down the ladder. Koko followed, then stopped, waiting for Mallory.

It was now or never, she realized, bracing herself for what she had to do. "I—I'm coming."

Eli tugged her into his arms and slammed the trap door shut.

Mallory gulped in air. "Eli?"

He didn't let go of her hand. "I'm here. Do you have your phone?"

"It's in my jacket pocket," she said, taking deep breaths and visualizing the ocean.

"Find the flashlight," he said. "I need to let go of your hand, okay?"

She squeezed his warm fingers. "Okay."

"Turn on your flashlight app. I'll send you ahead because we have to crawl."

"Ahead? No! I can't go any farther."

"I'll behind you. Koko first, then you, then me."

"How do I get out of here?"

"Follow Koko and keep moving. No matter what, keep moving."

They heard voices echoing nearby. Someone was coming.

Mallory's spine burned with sweat. Her fleece-lined jacket felt like scratchy wool tearing at her skin. She blinked when she finally found the flashlight app on her phone. Wiping away damp hair, she searched for Eli.

"I'm here," he said, crouching against the beamed ceiling. "Just leaving some barriers like rocks and old beams to throw them off. Mallory, you can do this. Take deep breaths and remember, Koko and I have you." Then he touched a hand to her face. "And God has all of us."

Mallory let those sweet words take control. "I can do this," she kept whispering. Then she got down on the cold cement floor. "I'm ready."

"Koko, go," she said with as much force as she could muster.

Koko looked back once and then he got down on his belly and began to crawl forward, coming up here and there to get better angles. Mallory did the same, her jeans digging into the hard surface, her boots scraping against the wood-framed walls. Dirt and rocks fell against her hair, cobwebs tickled her hands and cheeks. But she kept crawling. The voices behind them became more distant.

With each inch they took, she prayed for God to bring her out of the darkness. Eli held his light high, so she could see ahead. She kept her phone in one hand, holding it up to protect it, and so Koko had some light.

"How long?" she asked on a shudder.

"Another twenty yards or so," Eli said. "We'll come out in the back of the training yard. Near the building. Hopefully, we can make it inside."

The training yard—bright, open, safe. She'd be there soon.

"Koko, you're so good. You're doing great." If she praised her partner, she'd forget her own fears.

The K-9 never wavered. Koko knew his job. He understood duty and reward. She had to do the same.

"Up ahead," Eli called. "I'll get the hatch open."

"Okay." She gulped, hoping to find air. But her throat was so tight she could barely breathe. "Okay. Good boy, Koko. We're almost there." Her words were raspy and distant.

"Look up," Eli told her. "It should be right there."

Mallory lifted her head and shined the phone light on the ceiling. "I see it."

"I'm coming around," he said as he squeezed close to her.

Before he stood to open the hatch, he tugged her close. "Mallory, you are one of the bravest people I know."

She held tightly to him, his warmth, his scent, his nearness, giving her strength. "Thank you, Eli. I do trust you. I always have."

"Good, because you're gonna be seeing a lot more of me from now on."

Then he moved her aside, slipped around Koko and went to work on getting them out of the tunnel.

Mallory realized something as she watched him. She hadn't had a panic attack. And she waited, taking more breaths, while Eli pushed at the round hatch. Then she heard a creaking sound as someone above opened the hatch and stared down at them.

Someone who wasn't a member of the K-9 team.

"Please, come on out," the man said. When Eli turned back, the man leaned in, his features craggy and haggard. His gun pointed on them. "I insist."

Koko growled low behind Mallory. "Silent," she whispered. Eli glanced back. Koko knew this man wasn't their friend.

Eli turned to her. "Just do as he says." She nodded, her eyes moving to Koko, now hidden behind her.

Then Eli's chin jutted out in response. Giving her one last glance, he went up the ladder, and prayed he could somehow get them out of this.

"I'm guessing you're Red Graystone," he said, glancing around at the quiet yard as he took in the cold air and clumps of old snow. No one about.

Did this man take everyone hostage? He checked the main building. No fire. No activity. Lockdown?

"You'd guess correctly," the man said. He had a red beard and red hair.

Eli almost laughed. "Amarok?"

The man only grunted. "Don't try anything. I've got snipers trained on your head."

"Of course, you do. But no way you got them inside this compound. The explosions were a distraction, right?"

Big Wolf grinned. "I heard you'd been snooping around. I have kids who know how to track anything on the internet."

"You mean, *hack* anything on the internet."

The man waved his gun. "Track, hack. That rhymes."

"What do you want?" Eli asked, thinking of ways to stall the man.

"I *wanted* to get on with my Christmas plans, but now that's not possible. Give me the woman who's hiding down there," Big Wolf shouted as he leaned over the hatch. "Now, lady."

Eli gritted his teeth. *Mallory, just do as he asks.*

She slowly came up the ladder. Eli checked her with a warning glance, then watched the man with the gun before searching the area. Where was everyone?

His eye caught someone on top of headquarters. Someone in an Alaska State Trooper blue jacket. One of theirs!

Then he noticed a firetruck parked down the street. And an EMT bus. A flash from a window told him the team might be here, after all. But what were they waiting for?

Mallory was halfway out when Big Wolf grabbed her. "Let go of me," she shouted, twisting away. Then she called, "Attack!"

Eli took that as his cue. He let out a yell and headbutted Big Wolf, sending him to the ground. Koko took over from there, snarling and biting so hard that Big Wolf screamed in agony.

Shots hit the ground nearby, but Eli weaved and dodged away, pushing Mallory down.

Eli twisted and grabbed Big Wolf's gun out of his hand and dragged the man up. Koko still held his leg. "Mallory, stay down."

She complied. Then, once he knew she was out of harm's way, Eli held Big Wolf like a giant shield, using the man's weapon. Pressing it into Red Graystone's ample chest, he said, "Tell your men to back off."

Big Wolf grunted and signaled. "Get this mutt off me."

Then everything happened at once. The doors to the training center flew open and officers and dogs stormed out. Eli heard shots from the main building and dropped down with Mallory.

In a matter of seconds, Hunter McCord had

Red Graystone in cuffs, his K-9 partner, Juneau, barking and snarling. Eli gave the man's weapon to Hunter.

Then they heard screams. A woman held a weapon as she ran out the back door of the training building, officers behind her. She lifted the pistol and shot twice. Red Graystone fell to the ground, bleeding. Then he went still.

"Who's that?" Eli asked Hunter as he helped Mallory up.

"Mrs. Matson," Hunter replied. "We had her in for questioning. Looks like she grabbed a gun. He killed her daughter and her husband's dead, too. Poor woman."

Eli stood and took in the scene. A family torn apart. A gang leader dead. So many lives ruined. But they'd done it. They'd taken them down.

Mallory fell into Eli's arms. "Are you all right?"

He held one hand on her hair and the other around her waist. "Yes. You?"

"I'm fine. I made it through the dark, Eli."

He grinned. "You sure did." Then he leaned down and kissed her while the team finished rounding up the snipers. "Let's get inside," he said, dragging her close. "I promise we're going to stay in for the rest of winter. Koko, come."

SEVENTEEN

A week later, Eli and Mallory rushed around the kitchen of his new rental finishing up the Christmas meal they'd planned for the K-9 team.

"Okay, turkey's ready, ham's ready and we have sides," he said, grinning at Mallory over his shoulder.

"And everyone's bringing more sides and lots of desserts," Mallory replied, her grin as big as his.

He glanced out the big window over the sink, the distant mountains gleaming. He missed his cabin, but this one was nice enough for now. The cabin he'd lived in for years was just a shell now. But the whole team had volunteered to help him rebuild. Everyone here did that—someone knew someone who could do this or that and pretty soon, people got the help they needed. Like rebuilding a cabin out of real logs and real sweat labor.

Eli couldn't wait. He'd drawn up a new blueprint with more room, so Aidan could always have a place when he needed it. He planned to transfer to a local college in Anchorage. He and Harrison Seaver, Bettina's grandson, had become fast friends.

The main renovations would depend on Mallory.

He turned and found her and Koko staring at him.

"What?"

"You have that dreamy expression on your face," she said. "Koko are I are wondering what you're thinking?"

He grabbed her hand and tugged her to the sofa, the fire roaring in front of them, the Christmas tree winking at him.

"I love you," he said.

"You've told me that several times since—"

"Since we almost died. And I know you think I'll change my mind now that the adrenaline's settled down and you've argued all the science regarding that. But Mallory, my heart knows what my heart knows."

She giggled, a sound he loved. "Your heart is a mess, but I love that mess, and I love you."

"Wait, *what*? You love me?"

She touched a hand to his face. "You know I do."

"But you had all these roadblocks—our age

differences, our working together, your family, my family, the world, darkness."

She put a finger to his lips. "You're my light, Eli. My shining knight, all lit up like that Christmas tree."

He shrugged. "You make me light up."

"And my parents are impressed that we brought down a secretive robbery ring."

"I'm impressed, too," he said with another shrug. "I think the first dent came when you walloped that guy with a big limb and then Koko left a deep scar in his leg."

Koko woofed a quiet, "Yep, I did that."

Eli tugged her close. "Say it again?"

"My parents are impressed?"

"No."

"I love you?"

"Yeah, that."

Then he kissed her and pulled a gift out of his pocket. "I had planned to give you this—"

She grabbed the red box. *"Now?"*

"Yeah, now."

Mallory tore through the wrapping and then opened the black velvet box. Then she gasped. "Eli?"

The diamond solitaire sparkled like an ornament. "You don't have to say yes now."

"Yes, yes, I do," she said. "We'll figure out everything else. But I love you and I'm not going to let you go."

Eli put the ring on her finger and kissed her again. "We make a good team."

"We sure do."

Koko put his head down on his paws, his dark eyes bright. His work here was obviously done.

Then the doorbell rang, and everyone started piling in, carrying food and gifts.

Aidan came in with a big teddy bear and handed it to them.

"Hey, where's your stuff?" Mallory asked. "I thought you'd be staying here with Eli for a while."

The colonel and her K-9, Denali, came in. She handed her gifts off to someone and nodded at Aidan. "Well, tell them."

Aidan held his hands out. "I love both of you, but Lorenza offered to let me hang out at her place through the holidays. She said to save you the hassle, Eli. And hey, she likes me."

Colonel Gallo thumped him on the head with her fingers. "Yeah, that and someone needs to look after you. You did save their lives, you know."

Aidan did a fist pump. "I made a few calls. Got a few people off the most-wanted list."

Eli shook his head. "You'd make a great police officer."

"If he doesn't keep the big head," Lorenza said.

"I'm going to *be* a police officer," Aidan declared, running a hand through his hair. "I'm changing to criminal justice courses, and as soon as I get out of college, I'm going to sign up for the police academy. K-9 unit."

Lorenza said, "Mercy on us all." But she beamed like a proud mother.

Eli hugged Mallory close. All of their coworkers were here. The whole team together, with the people they loved.

"Hey," Lorenza called out in typical colonel fashion, "I need to say something."

Everyone gathered around.

"We've had an exciting year," she said. "But we made it through alive." After applause, she glanced around the room. "You all matter to me. I'm proud to be your leader. And I just wanted to wish everyone a Merry Christmas."

Will Stryker called out, "Hey, Colonel, Mallory's wearing a rock on her left hand."

Lorenza turned to Mallory. "Well, show me."

Mallory held up her hand, her blush making Eli smile.

Aidan stepped forward. "She's supposed to wait for me."

Everyone laughed at that and Eli grabbed him and knuckled him. "She's with me. Always."

Then he kissed Mallory to prove his point.

Koko barked and danced. He had decided he'd stay with Mallory when the team didn't need him to fight bad guys. Then he ran off to play with his K-9 friends.

Mallory and Eli stood watching. Aidan walked up and handed Eli a gift bag. "I grabbed this—that night when everything happened. I hid it outside your other cabin under a bench."

Eli opened the bag and pulled out a golden tree angel. "The angel Bettina gave me," he said, his eyes burning.

"I remembered how much this ornament meant to you," Aidan replied in a husky tone. "Oh, and Bettina and Harrison said to tell you both hello. They're celebrating at the hospice place. But call them later."

"Thank you," Eli said. "Thank you."

He hurried and placed the angel on the tree he and Mallory had decorated last night. "Now it's Christmas."

"This is our family, Eli," she said, her hand in his.

Eli tugged her close. "You'll never be in the dark again, Mallory. I promise."

She squeezed his hand. "And neither will you."

* * * * *

Dear Reader,

I really enjoyed writing this quirky story to bring the Alaskan K-9 Unit series to an end. I loved these two characters and considered them a challenge since they technically weren't K-9 officers. But I begged my sweet, adorable, always accommodating (:)) editor to let me write their story. I'm so glad she agreed.

I hope you've enjoyed Eli and Mallory's story. Koko says, "Woof, woof."

I believe God uses the least expected people to do the hardest jobs at times, and He rejoices when they come through and know that He's with them.

He's with all of us, so I hope you have a great Christmas and the best of New Year's!

Until next time, may the angels watch over you. Always!

Lenora Worth

Get 4 FREE REWARDS!

We'll send you 2 FREE Books plus 2 FREE Mystery Gifts.

Harlequin Heartwarming Larger-Print books will connect you to uplifting stories where the bonds of friendship, family and community unite.

FREE Value Over $20

YES! Please send me 2 FREE Harlequin Heartwarming Larger-Print novels and my 2 FREE mystery gifts (gifts worth about $10 retail). After receiving them, if I don't wish to receive any more books, I can return the shipping statement marked "cancel." If I don't cancel, I will receive 4 brand-new larger-print novels every month and be billed just $5.74 per book in the U.S. or $6.24 per book in Canada. That's a savings of at least 21% off the cover price. It's quite a bargain! Shipping and handling is just 50¢ per book in the U.S. and $1.25 per book in Canada.* I understand that accepting the 2 free books and gifts places me under no obligation to buy anything. I can always return a shipment and cancel at any time. The free books and gifts are mine to keep no matter what I decide.

161/361 HDN GNPZ

Name (please print)

Address   Apt. #

City   State/Province   Zip/Postal Code

Email: Please check this box ☐ if you would like to receive newsletters and promotional emails from Harlequin Enterprises ULC and its affiliates. You can unsubscribe anytime.

Mail to the Harlequin Reader Service:
IN U.S.A.: P.O. Box 1341, Buffalo, NY 14240-8531
IN CANADA: P.O. Box 603, Fort Erie, Ontario L2A 5X3

Want to try 2 free books from another series! Call 1-800-873-8635 or visit www.ReaderService.com.

HW21R2